Saddles and Spurs

Veteran gunfighter Tom Dix and his partner, retired lawman Dan Shaw, are taking their prize bull to California to put it up for sale. But even before they set out from Cheyenne aboard the long freight train things do not run smoothly.

With their old friend Wild Bill Hickok in tow, they soon discover that their journey will be blighted. With each and every one of Hickok's enemies wanting revenge, Dix must again rely upon his unmatched gun skills if they are to have any chance of survival.

Saddles and Spurs

WALT KEENE

A Black Horse Western

ROBERT HALE · LONDON

© Walt Keene 2005
First published in Great Britain 2005

ISBN 0 7090 7836 6

Robert Hale Limited
Clerkenwell House
Clerkenwell Green
London EC1R 0HT

Typeset by
Derek Doyle & Associates, Shaw Heath.
Printed and bound in Great Britain by
Antony Rowe Limited, Wiltshire

Dedicated with respect to my friends,
Joanne and Monte Hale.
'Shoot low, they might be crawling!'

ONE

The dozens of saloons and gaming-houses within the boundaries of Cheyenne were busy. The stock-pens to both sides of the railtracks were filled to overflowing with thousands of cattle waiting to be transported East. A lot of money had changed hands during the previous few days and it had already started to burn holes in the pockets of the dust-caked cowboys who had driven the herds hundreds of miles to reach this famed town. Most behaved themselves but not all. After months on the trail eating dust, a lot of the mostly illiterate youngsters wanted only two things and Cheyenne supplied them both. There was always an abundance of hard liquor and females of easy virtue in the towns which had grown like weeds along the rail tracks.

Trouble also festered like open wounds when so many hot-headed strangers arrived in town at the same time. Fist-fights were so numerous that the law ignored the majority of them. They even ignored the sound of gunshots, fearing the wrath of the larger teams of cattle-drovers.

Cheyenne was no place for those of a nervous nature when the trail herds arrived with their thousands of steers and dozens of cowboys.

Few of the more respectable locals dared venture out on to the boardwalks after dark when the town was this busy. But the tall man with the flat-brimmed hat was neither respectable nor local.

To some he was a hero. To others a brutal killer. To all who knew of James Butler Hickok, he was Wild Bill. Not a man to tangle with if you liked living. He had ridden on both sides of the law and managed to survive.

He locked his hotel door and slid the key into his silk vest pocket and then started along the narrow corridor towards the staircase that led down to the wide foyer.

As he reached the top of the stairs, he paused, rested one of his hands on the mahogany rails and studied what lay below him carefully. Hickok had a way of drawing the wrong sort of attention from those who did not have the brains to recognize the man who was known throughout the world as the infamous Wild Bill. It was something that he had grown used to over the years since he had first become famous as a war hero.

But those heroic years were far behind him now. Since his factual and fictional exploits had been written up in dozens of dime novels, Hickok had found himself unable to hold down a steady job for very long.

His flamboyant appearance did not help. It drew trouble like flies to an outhouse. His hooded eyes, untamed moustache and long flowing hair which hung half-way down his broad back was something from another time. It harked back to when he and several of his equally famous friends had lived as mountain men and hunted buffalo for the bounty on their heads. Yet Hickok had not lasted long even as a buffalo-hunter.

It was a curse to be plagued by boredom. Nothing that life had so far thrown at him had managed to satisfy his insatiable appetite for excitement and adventure. He was a creature without a soul who drowned his sorrows in countless bottles of whiskey and the arms of any willing female. He had grown to believe the stories that were written about him even when he knew they were untrue. He wanted to be the character the dime novelists wrote about so badly that it tainted everything else in his real life.

Hickok had worked hard to become a living legend and had, for the most part, succeeded. His gun skills were probably far better than those of most so-called gunslingers. His expertise at poker was also something which had never let him down during his life roaming around the West.

Yet it was not easy being Wild Bill Hickok.

There was never a solitary moment of any day when he could relax fully and forget that a lot of people wanted him dead. To kill someone like Hickok was a coup that could make someone instantly famous.

So many had tried.

So many had died.

Hickok had been a scout, a gunfighter, a lawman, a bounty hunter, a gambler and a lot of other things for most of the previous twenty years and yet none of it meant a thing. He knew that what remained of his colourful life would be challenged almost daily by those whom he had yet to encounter. Unlike his friend William F. Cody, he had no business skills to match his gun skills and had never managed to truly profit from his undoubted fame.

For all his glory, he was little more than a living target.

The one thing that had never altered was the fact that he remained an enigma. Someone to be feared and yet admired. For even those who despised Hickok and what he stood for could not fail to admit that he was a man who could be relied upon to be there if you needed him. For he did not fear death like more rational people.

Hickok inhaled deeply and descended the carpeted staircase toward the half-dozen figures within the hotel lobby. Every eye was on the elegant man with the two pearl-handed guns that poked out across his flat stomach. Hickok, unlike nearly all his fellow gunfighters, never wore ordinary holsters that hung on the thighs. He had designed his own shooting-rig. The holsters were almost level with his gunbelt in a manner that only an expert of the notorious cross-draw could use.

The gun-grips jutted out like the horns of a steer. They warned everyone of the deadly danger which faced them.

'Good evening, Mr Hickok,' the desk clerk said, nodding at the long-legged man as he strode across the carpeted floor towards the door and the lantern-lit streets of Cheyenne. 'Have a nice evening.'

Hickok did not reply.

He stepped out on to the boardwalk and looked up and down the wide, busy street which was illuminated by scores of storefronts and street-lanterns. Men, women and children still scurried around from one store to another, as was their daily ritual.

Horsemen of every colour and creed roamed up and down the dusty thoroughfare astride their horses and mules. A stagecoach came hurriedly along the street pulled by a team of six lathered-up sorrels. It stopped outside the Wells Fargo stage depot directly opposite the tall man.

Hickok wondered if it were possible to die of boredom. He put a long cigar between his teeth and bit off its tip. He spat the brown remnant out and then gripped the cigar firmly in the corner of his mouth. He pulled a match from his vest pocket and ran his left thumbnail across its top. Hickok sucked the flame in and then blew out a long line of smoke.

'Howdy, Mr Hickok!'

'Evenin', Wild Bill!'

After only a few minutes, he had lost count of how many people had greeted him as they crossed his path. He wondered how much friendliness was spawned by fear rather than respect.

The noise of a tinny piano drew his attention to his right and he started to walk towards it. He had already gambled in half the town's saloons and gaming-halls since he had arrived here a month earlier and was showing a good profit. Few card-players ever questioned his honesty.

Yet it was not the money which had kept him here since he had helped his two friends Tom Dix and Dan Shaw defeat the powerful men who had run the deadly rustler-gang known as the Brand Burners.

Cheyenne had proved to be a place where rough diamonds such as himself could ply their various skills and trades without much interference from those who wore tin stars on their chests as he had done at various times during his colourful existence.

Hickok's reputation alone kept the sheriff and his deputies at bay. They wanted nothing to do with the figure who walked their streets in his long tail-coat.

The tall man pulled the cigar from his mouth, tapped the ash and looked up at the sign above the porch overhang.

The Diamond Back saloon was far bigger than most of its fellow drinking-holes. It was also noisier. The saloon was filled with cowboys spending their hard-earned wages on whiskey and women as well as those who profited from the cattle auctions and played keno and poker. The piano sounded out of tune to the tall Hickok as he walked to the swing-doors.

The wiser of the men who saw Hickok approaching the saloon doors moved well out of the way. They had seen this tall, pale-faced man many times during the previous month and knew that he had used the guns he sported to deadly effect.

Smoke hung at eye-level across the saloon. He noticed the females in their low-cut brightly dyed dresses moving from one potential customer to the next like bees seeking pollen. A balcony encircled the saloon and was busy as some of the bargiris led their clients to and from the half-dozen rooms.

Wild Bill entered and strode across the busy sawdust-covered floorboards until he reached the long, damp bar. He rested a boot on the brass rail and stared around the faces which surrounded him.

His hooded eyes searched the faces as if trying

to see which if any of them posed a threat. He had long become known for always sitting with his back to the wall for fear of being backshot by someone not brave enough to face him.

It had become a habit of which he was no longer aware. But even this was no guarantee that someone might simply draw and shoot. He had often wondered if his life might end because of a lucky shot.

His eyes burned across the features of men and women alike inside the Diamond Back. All turned away as if fearing to face this living legend for more than a mere heartbeat. Hickok grabbed the arm of the prettiest of the bargirls and dragged her towards him. She looked up into his smooth features and smiled.

'You want a good time, Wild Bill?' she asked coyly.

He pulled her closer, bent down and kissed her bright-red lips.

'I'll need your services later,' he said as he slipped a few silver coins down her cleavage and stroked her powdered skin.

'All night?' ghe smiled.

He dropped another few coins down the fragrant gap between her swollen breasts and nodded.

'What'll it be, Bill?' the bartender asked.

'Whiskey, barkeep!' Hickok replied, tossing two silver dollars at the man. 'A bottle.'

'Sure thing.' The bartender turned and grabbed a bottle off the shelf behind him and then paused. He replaced it and picked up a better brand.

Hickok nodded as the bottle was placed before him with a small thimble-glass over its cork stopper.

'This the good stuff?'

'The best, Bill!'

Hickok removed the glass and placed it down on the wet counter. He then pulled the cork with his teeth and spat it at the floor. He filled the glass with the amber liquor and downed it swiftly. Hickok filled the glass again.

'I thought you'd have left town by now, Bill,' the bartender said as he continued to serve other customers. 'After all them varmints you and your pals shot.'

The tall man eyed his questioner.

'Do I make you nervous, partner?'

The bartender felt sweat run down his spine.

'You could say that,' he admitted.

'Good.' Hickok picked up his bottle and glass and made his way towards the closest card-game. There were four men seated at the round green-baize table.

He stared at them.

One by one the men looked up from the cards in their hands at the tall thin figure who loomed over them. The oldest looking of the card-players cleared his throat.

'You want to sit in, Wild Bill?' he asked.

Hickok nodded.

'Only if I can sit with my back to the wall, gentlemen.'

The men all looked into each others' eyes. Silently two of the players moved up one chair, leaving an empty seat so that Hickok could sit with his back protected by the wall. He walked around the table and sat down. The card-players continued their game until one of the men scooped all the chips up before him.

Hickok placed his bottle and glass on the table.

'This is a high-stake table, Wild Bill,' one of the other players said bluntly.

Hickok pulled out a roll of bills. He peeled off four hundred-dollar bills and tossed them at the man.

'Chips!' he demanded.

The man carefully pushed four tall stacks of chips towards Hickok.

'Reckon you got enough there?'

Hickok smiled. 'I reckon I won't need any more.'

Suddenly two young cowboys staggered out of the crowd and drew their guns. They fired up at the high vaulted ceiling, then re-holstered their weapons. They were about to head back to the bar when they noticed Hickok staring at them with narrowed eyes. They pushed a few other men aside, then looked across the table at the seated Hickok.

'You better head on out of here, boys,' Wild Bill said. He poured another glass of whiskey for himself and downed it in one swallow. 'I don't like trash eyeing me.'

'Look at that critter, Jeb!' The first cowboy laughed pointing at the drinking Hickok. 'All duded up like some fancy Easterner. Damned if he don't look like he's wearing face-powder.'

'Must be one of them sissy actors we heard tell about!' The other laughed as both men forced their way through the saloon's customers closer to the table. 'How come ya hair is so long? Does ya want to be a girl?'

One of the poker-players turned to the pair of drunken cowboys and stared hard at them.

'Get out of here, boys!' he ordered. 'You'll end up dead if ya don't.'

The smile disappeared from the face of the first cowboy. He looked down at the older man and poked a finger into his left cheek.

'Shut up, ya fat bastard!' he spat. 'I was talking to the stupid-lookin' idiot with the long hair.'

Another of the seated card-players interrupted.

'Get out of here, you young idiots. Don't you know who this is? This is Wild Bill!'

'I never heard of anyone called Wild Bill. All we know is that he looks kinda girlie to us!' The cowboy named Jeb laughed loudly.

James Butler Hickok finished another drink. He rose up and stood across the table from the cowboys. There was fire in the eyes of the deadly gunfighter.

'You'd better run away damn fast,' he warned. 'Or I'll surely kill you both.'

Both cowboys stared at the immaculate figure of Hickok. They had never set eyes upon anyone who dressed like him before. Yet they did not recognize the deadly man. Few of their kind ever learned to read so his reported exploits meant nothing to them. All they could see was a figure that was ripe for mocking. Their drunken eyes traced up and down him. To them he was far too well-groomed to be a real man worthy of fearing.

'Are you sure you got them guns the right way around?' the second cowboy mocked. 'Reckon girls shoot side-saddle, huh?'

'I'm dead sure my guns are the right way around,' Wild Bill said in a low drawl. He flexed his fingers above his gun-grips. 'You want to try me out, boys? You wanna draw on me?'

The first cowboy adjusted his own gunbelt and stroked the handle of his gun.

'Reckon we'll have to learn this critter a few manners.'

'He needs someone to learn him OK, Jeb.' the other agreed. 'Back in Texas we don't cotton to men with long hair.'

The rest of the poker-players pushed their chairs away from the table and moved quickly out of the line of fire. Hickok did not seem to notice their departure. His unblinking eyes were fixed on the two dusty cowboys six feet away from him.

Both cowboys grinned and stood square on to Hickok.

'Go for ya guns, missy!' one laughed.

'After you, boy!' Hickok said calmly.

The cowboys went for their guns.

Before either had managed to draw their weapons out of their holsters, Hickok had cross-drawn his gleaming guns. He held them both at arm's length and aimed at each of the cowboys' heads.

'I'd stop now unless you want to die!' Hickok warned loudly.

The cowboys continued to pull their guns clear of their holsters and raise them in the direction of the slim steely-eyed gunfighter.

'Get the varmint!' one shouted.

Hickok squeezed both his triggers. His aim was equally deadly with both guns. The cowboys were lifted off their feet and crashed into the abandoned tables behind them. Glasses shattered as both bodies slid on to the sawdust. Hickok remained still like a statue as smoke drifted from the barrels of his weapons.

'Drag them out of here and dump them in the alley,' the bartender said as he rushed to the blood-covered floor with a bucket of fresh sawdust in his hands. He scattered the sawdust over the bloody floor as four hefty men dragged the dead cowboys out through the swing-doors. 'That ought to do it. OK, folks, the trouble's over.'

Hickok slid his guns back into their holsters, then sat down and smiled at the nervous card-players. Slowly, the four men resumed their seats. Sweat dripped from all their faces. Wild Bill lifted the deck of cards up and started to shuffle.

'My deal?' he asked.

The card-players nodded.

TWO

It was almost midnight when the two riders arrived in the still bustling Cheyenne. They were looking for the one man who might be able to offer them some advice. Tom Dix and Dan Shaw had heard about the shooting in the Diamond Back saloon as they tied their mounts' reins to the hitching-poles outside the livery stables. The long, winding main street seemed to buzz with people who could not talk about anything else except Hickok's blood-thirsty slayings. Yet the two ranchers knew there had to be more to it than just a brutal double killing.

Both men knew that if Hickok had killed some-one the odds were that the varmints required killing. The tall gunfighter never wasted energy or bullets.

They meandered along the twisting boardwalks until they saw the excited crowd gathered outside the saloon.

'Reckon Wild Bill must still be in that saloon for

there to be such a crowd outside, Dixie,' Shaw said as they stepped down on to the dusty street and made their way towards the Diamond Back.

'Sure hope he's in there,' Dix replied. He paused to let a buckboard cross his path. 'I'd hate to have to waste all night trying to track him down.'

Dan Shaw smiled.

'Yep, there sure are a lot of soiled doves in Cheyenne.'

'And Bill knows most of them.' Dix grinned, stepped up on to the boardwalk and started to force his way through the crowd of people which had gathered and who were trying to look over the swing-doors at something that was happening inside the still busy drinking-hole.

Both men managed to force the nosy onlookers apart and reach the swing-doors. They pushed them open, entered and then stopped to try and get their bearings. There were more folks to their right so they aimed their pointed boots in that direction.

There were so many people within the drinking-hole that it seemed impossible for anyone to move. The crowd was mumbling as men gave commentary to what they were witnessing. It sounded like a herd of nervous steers.

Tom Dix turned and looked at Shaw.

'He must be over there, partner.'

Dan looked at the backs of the men before

them. Each of them seemed to be pointing their heads in exactly the same direction looking for something that they had yet to set eyes upon.

Tom Dix nodded and then forced his way through the crowd with his pal close on his spurred heels. He kept hauling men aside until he saw what all the fuss was about.

The gleaming marshal's star pinned to the vest of the broad, overweight figure standing beside the poker-table flashed in the light of a swaying lantern above the card-players.

Dix looked at the table. There was a stack of chips in its centre. Two players besides Hickok remained in the game.

The marshal had a small notebook and a well-licked pencil with which he was vainly trying to take notes about the earlier shootings. By the redness of his cheeks, he was getting nowhere real fast.

Dix rested his gloved hands on the back of an empty chair and nodded to Hickok. The gunfighter briefly removed his smouldering cigar from his mouth.

'Dixie!' Hickok said before returning the cigar back between his teeth.

Shaw stood beside Dix and looked at the frustrated lawman who was trying to get statements from the saloon's customers. Yet it seemed that, for all his questioning, all the fat man got in return were shrugs.

'You winning, James Butler?' Dix asked.

The hooded eyes of the man flashed from the large stack of chips to his friend's face. There was no reply.

'I'll call ya, Wild Bill,' the man opposite Hickok piped up.

'Can you beat three queens?' Hickok asked.

The man tossed his cards into the middle of the table and stood. There was a look on his face that Hickok had seen many times before.

'Damn it, Bill. You are the luckiest critter I've ever played cards with.' He stormed away.

Wild Bill Hickok pushed the chips to the other card-player who had been acting as banker. He smiled.

'Cash them up, friend,' he said, pushing his cards into the deep pocket of his frock-coat.

The man quickly counted the chips, then peeled off six hundred-dollar bills and a quantity of smaller bills. Hickok plucked the money out of the man's hand and stood up. He slid the six larger denomination bills into his vest pocket and held on to the others.

'At last!' the marshal said as he realized the poker-game was over. 'I want to know what happened here earlier, Bill. Folks reckon you shot two cowpokes dead. Is that right?'

Hickok stared down at the shorter man. He had a belly that hung over the buckle of his gunbelt.

'Are you a real marshal?' Hickok asked through

a cloud of smoke. 'I've never seen a fat marshal before.'

'I could arrest you right now, Hickok!' the marshal said. 'I have the word of a dozen souls that you shot two men earlier.'

'I wouldn't try it,' Hickok warned in a low drawl.

'You don't scare me, Hickok!'

Hickok grinned.

'Fat and dumb? You ain't gonna live too long, son. If I was you I'd find me a job that suits me better.'

Tom Dix and Dan Shaw moved around the table and flanked their old pal as Hickok spread the smaller bills from his poker winnings out in his hand like a fan. He waved them above his head and threw them at the law officer.

The crowd went wild as they all tried to grab the floating paper-money. There was a pitiful yelp. The rotund lawman disappeared beneath the scores of people.

Wild Bill walked to the bar and stared across at the smiling female whom he had already paid. She was still waiting. He then diverted his attention to his two companions.

'You looking for me, boys?'

'Yep.' Dan nodded. 'We need your help, Bill.'

Tom Dix looked at the poker-faced gunfighter.

'Did you really have three queens, James Butler?'

'Nope.'

'But you asked that man if he could beat three queens.' Dan Shaw sighed.

Hickok smiled.

'Exactly. I didn't say I had three little ladies, Dan. I just asked that old man if he could beat three queens. Understand?'

'Oh.' Shaw nodded and rested his elbows on the bar.

'A simple enough question.' Dix raised a finger to the bartender. The man started towards them. 'It ain't your fault that he misunderstood your meaning, is it.'

Hickok dropped his cigar on to the floor and trod on it. 'He folded too quick, Dixie!'

'Didn't even wait to see your hand.'

'Exactly.'

The marshal managed to force himself from the midst of the men and women who were fighting over the money that Hickok had discarded. His coat was covered in sawdust and he had lost his notebook and pencil. He waved a finger at the tall Hickok angrily.

'I'm starting to get mighty angry with you, Hickok!' he snapped. 'You wouldn't like me when I'm angry!'

'I don't like you anyway.' Wild Bill sighed.

'You don't understand do you? You're in a whole lot of trouble, Mr Hickok!' The eyes of the marshal narrowed as the finger waved even faster. 'Hanging trouble!'

Hickok nodded and then clenched his right hand into a fist at his side.

'You're starting to really annoy me, little man!'

'We'll see how annoyed you get when I throw you in jail. We'll see how annoyed you get when you stand trial for murder!'

'Self-defence, Marshal!' the bartender said from across the bar counter. 'I seen it all.'

'What?' the lawman gasped as his attention was drawn to the man with the apron around him. 'What you say, barkeep?'

'Those two young cowboys come in here shooting their guns off like nobody's business. Wild Bill asked them to stop and they drew on him. He had to shoot them. I reckon that's self-defence, ain't it?'

The marshal's face went pale as his jaw dropped.

'You'd swear to that?'

'Sure thing.' The barteder nodded. 'Get me Good Book. I'll swear on it!'

The marshal looked up at the smiling face of Hickok.

'To think that you were once a marshal. You should be ashamed. What kind of life is this?'

'You really are annoying.' Hickok lowered his chin and then threw his fist hard into the lawman's midriff. The marshal gasped and buckled. Hickok then grabbed him by the collar and belt and pulled him with all his strength. The marshal's head hit the side of the bar counter. There was a cracking sound a moment before the stunned figure fell to the floor.

'Self-defence!' The bartender chuckled.

The entire bar erupted into laughter.

'What exactly is it you want, Dixie?' Hickok asked as he led the two men out of the saloon into the lantern-lit street. 'Talk fast, boys. I'm a tad busy. I have a filly in there I have to service.'

'Is she in need of spiritual guidance, Bill?' Dan asked leaning against a wooden upright.

Wild Bill Hickok smiled broadly.

'Something like that, brother Daniel.'

THREE

The tall gunfighter struck a match and lit a long, thin cigar. He rested his shoulder against one of the wooden uprights outside the Diamond Back saloon and studied the long street as his two friends moved to either side of him.

'We need to find a cattle buyer, James Butler.' Tom Dix sighed heavily.

Hickok's hooded eyes darted to the face of the man he had known for half his life. Even the flickering lantern-light of the saloon porch could not hide the regret in Dix's weathered features.

'How come?' Wild Bill asked.

Dix gritted his teeth and rested his gloved knuckles on the gun-grips of his matched Colts. He glanced at the floorboards before answering.

'Me and old Dan are broke, *amigo*,' he admitted. 'The bank wanted the money they loaned us repaid. With no herd to sell next year, we're stony.'

Hickok turned his head and looked at Shaw.

'That right, Dan?'

Dan Shaw nodded.

'Yep.'

Hickok was confused. He inhaled the acrid smoke and allowed it to fill his lungs as he tried to accept the blunt statement. He wondered how on earth they could be in financial trouble after he had helped them defeat the Brand Burners a month earlier.

'Didn't you get your steers back after we sorted out them rustlers and their crooked boss?'

Dix laughed. 'Only a handful.'

Hickok glanced down along the street. He could hear raised voices in the direction of the railtracks. Voices that seemed to be getting closer. His attention then returned to Dix.

'I don't understand, Dixie.'

Tom Dix smiled. 'Those Brand Burners did a real good job on our steers, Wild Bill. By the time we went through the stock-pens, we only managed to find five of our steers that had not had their brands changed by them rustlers. The others were lost among the thousands of other steers. Those men sure knew how to handle their branding-irons OK.'

'So all you got left is five steers?'

'Nope,' Dan interrupted. 'We had to sell them to cover some of our debts. All we got left now is our pedigree white-faced bull. The bank ain't gonna get their hands on him.'

'But you still own the ranch,' Hickok said. 'That

has to be worth something, don't it?'

'Not a plug nickel, Bill,' Shaw replied. 'It was mortgaged and the bank pulled the rug from under us. They sure know how to suck blood.'

'So all you got left is the bull?'

'He's worth a tidy sum to the right folks,' Dix said. 'Trouble is we don't know the right folks. Do you?'

The noise down the street was growing louder. Wild Bill sucked on his cigar thoughtfully and then stepped down into the street. He looked over his shoulder at his friends.

'C'mon, boys. I got me a wire to send.'

Dix and Dan followed Hickok across the street and along the boardwalk until they reached the telegraph office. The tall man opened the door and entered. The ranchers trailed him into the dimly lit office. They closed the door behind them and watched as the small telegraph-operator stared at Hickok open-mouthed.

'You're Wild Bill Hickok!' the small man gasped.

'I know!' Hickok nodded. 'That's Tom Dix.'

The man glanced at Dix and then back to the man with the flowing long hair that hung over his shoulders from under his hatband.

'I never heard of him, but I sure know who you are.'

'Take this message,' Hickok started.

'Wait.' The man licked the end of his pencil and readied himself over the sheet of yellow paper.

'OK. I'm ready.'

'To Kirby Jones. San Remo, California.' Wild Bill began.'Dear Kirby. Have pals with pedigree bull to sell. You want a bull with vinegar? Send offer. They will deliver beast. Your friend, Wild Bill.'

The man counted the words and then looked up at Hickok.

'That'll be three dollars and ten cents, sir.'

Wild Bill pulled out four silver dollars and placed them on the sheet of yellow paper.

'Send that right away, son. Bring the reply to the Diamond Back as soon as it arrives. I'll be upstairs with a lady.'

'Yes, sir!' The man almost saluted.

Hickok opened the office door again and led his friends out on to the dark porch. He stared across at the Diamond Back and sighed heavily.

'Damn,' he muttered.

Dix rubbed his chin and stared at the ten or more cowboys outside the saloon. They were angry and it showed. They were screaming for blood. Hickok's blood.

'Do you think them varmints might be pals of the two cowboys you shot earlier, James Butler?' Dix asked.

'Reckon so by the looks and sounds of it, Dixie.' Hickok tapped ash off his cigar. 'That's the trouble with folks you kill, they always got themselves friends or kin bent on getting even.'

Dix grabbed the arm of the tall, thoughtful gunfighter.

'Let's cut up this alley and take the long way back to your hotel. We don't have to get mixed up with them cowpokes. They're all fired up on cheap liquor. By tomorrow, when they've sobered up, they won't even recall the names of their pals.'

Hickok nodded.

'But I've got me a gal in that saloon waiting to earn the money I've already paid her, Dix. I can't let a bunch of cowboys get between me and her. Besides, it'd look as if I was scared of them dust-caked critters if I just turned and headed in the opposite direction, wouldn't it.'

Dan Shaw shook his head.

'There are too many of them, Bill.'

'No there ain't,' Hickok argued.

'You want me to back you up, James Butler?' Dix asked. He quickly checked that his guns were fully loaded before returning them to their holsters.

Wild Bill shook his head and pulled the cigar from his mouth. He flicked it away into the darkness.

'Thanks for the offer, Dixie. But this ain't nothing to do with you. I'll sort it out myself.'

Yet the choice of what to do next was not Hickok's to make. The cowboys were about to unleash their lust for revenge on the gunfighter and his pals.

'There he is!' one of the cowboys screamed out

at the top of his voice from outside the saloon. 'There's the long-haired dude who killed Jeb and Slim! Let's kill that bastard!'

'Kill him!' another shouted.

Suddenly the street was lit up with deafening gunfire as each of the cowboys drew his weapon and fired at exactly the same time.

Bullets ripped the outside of the telegraph office apart and showered the three startled men in a million hot splinters.

They all ducked and moved to the alley. Dix drew his guns, then ran to a water-trough and knelt down beside it. The street was filled with black, acrid gunsmoke.

'Can you see them?' Dix called out to his two pals.

With each backward step Dan and Wild Bill took searching for cover, Hickok squeezed off a bullet into the smoke. Red-hot tapers of lethal lead came at the three men from all sides as the cowboys fanned out and fired blindly.

Dan ducked behind a water-barrel and grabbed the tall gunfighter. He hauled Hickok down and shook his head.

'Don't you ever look for cover, Bill?' he asked as he dragged his own gun from its holster and cocked its hammer. 'Do you think that you're invisible or something?'

'I'm too skinny for most folks to hit, Dan.' Wild Bill grinned wryly as he reloaded the gun in his hands with bullets from his deep pockets. 'They're only cowpunchers. Most of their breed can't shoot straight anyways.'

Then a bullet cut its way out of the black smoke and tore the hat from Hickok's head. He touched the top of his scalp and then stared at the spots of blood on his fingertips.

'They're going to pay for that!'

'Easy, Bill!' Dan said. 'The bullet just nicked ya, that's all.'

'That was a fifty-dollar hat, Dan!' Wild Bill yelled. 'My best fifty-dollar hat!'

The furious gunfighter leapt to his feet and drew his other gun. He started to fire with one gun and then the other as he steadily moved forward. With each shot a cowboy was knocked off his feet. Hickok walked to the alley wall opposite and rested his shoulder against it as bullets ripped chunks of the wooden corner away.

Then he fired again with both Colts.

A pitiful scream filled the air.

Dix went to move from the trough when half a dozen bullets hit the side of it. Water started to squirt out as the gunfighter rose and ran towards the alley and his two friends.

Then four of the crazed cowboys raced out of the blinding gunsmoke and jumped on Dix. His boots slipped from under him and he fell. He hit the ground hard and felt both his guns explode into action as their hammers fell. The bullets cut up into one of the cowboys who twisted on his heels before crashing into the wall next to Dan Shaw.

Dan jumped to his feet when he saw the cowboys' guns aimed at his partner.

He fired. His bullet hit one of the cowboys high in the shoulder. He fell in agony.

Then Hickok stepped out of the shadows and blasted the other pair off Dix's back. He continued to stride back towards the main street into the choking gunsmoke.

Tom Dix staggered to his feet and cocked the hammers of his weaponry once more. The sound of five more shots echoed around Cheyenne.

Then there was silence.

As the night breeze blew the smoke away Dan and Dix saw Wild Bill Hickok standing in the middle of the street reloading his prized guns. He was surrounded by bodies of dead and wounded cowboys.

Dix and Dan walked to the tall man.

'You OK, James Butler?' Dix asked.

Hickok slid both guns into their holsters and looked at his companions.

'I need a drink, boys! C'mon. I'm buying.'

FOUR

Bats darted around the quiet streets of Cheyenne as they chased countless large moths which were attracted to the street-lanterns' glowing lights. It was nearly five and still dark outside the Diamond Back when the swing-doors flew open and the telegraph operator rushed in with the neatly folded scrap of paper in his hand. He took ten steps across the sawdust-covered floor and then stopped. The saloon was virtually empty apart from the sleeping bartender propped up on a high stool with his head resting on the wet counter top. His snores echoed around the wooden structure like the grunts of a wallowing pig. The telegraph operator spun on his heels, then spied the two ranchers. They were at a card-table in the saloon's furthest corner.

Tom Dix had chosen this spot for him and Dan to wait for their flamboyant friend, as it offered views of not only the Diamond Back's front entrance but also the two side doors, which led to alleys.

Dix had feared that there might be even more men bent on revenge and killing the famed Wild Bill Hickok. If there were, he and his friend would be ready. His worries had proved groundless and no one had tried to emulate the ill-fated actions of the cowboys.

The telegraph operator looked around the vast interior and then back to the two ranchers. He looked like someone that had arrived at a party which had long since ended.

Dix curled a finger at the small, panting man.

'Is that for Wild Bill?' he called out.

'Yes, sir.' The man nodded and then looked up at the doors above them in the landing walls. A few muffled noises could still be heard coming from behind them as some clients refused to quit until they had managed to get their money's worth. 'Is he up there?'

Dix smiled.

'Yep. He is.'

The man walked towards Dix and Dan with the telegraph message in his hand. He never took his eyes off the doors on the high landing.

'I ain't never been in here before,' he admitted coyly. 'Is it right about the bargirls?'

Dix cleared his throat.

'Yep.'

'Gee,' the man said as he reached the table.

'You've never been in this saloon before?' Dan asked curiously.

The man looked at the seated rancher.

'Truth is I ain't never been in any of the saloons in Cheyenne before. My ma is kinda strict and all. You know?'

Dan grinned.

'I know. I figure that the kind of female to be found in these places are not the sort you'd want to take home to meet your ma.'

The man raised both eyebrows.

'Why not, sir?'

'Most got things a man can catch. You need a good clean living gal, son. Maybe a school teacher or the like. Your ma would be proud if'n you took one of them home. The gals in here are a little soiled.'

'They wears paint and powder on their faces too!' the small man said.

'Yep!' Dan tried not to smile. 'And cheap perfume.'

'But they're friendly, I'm told.' The man looked wistful as if he might never discover the truth for himself. 'I hear that they're awful friendly.'

Dix glanced at his pal and then back at the man.

'It's only money that makes them friendly, son.'

'Reckon Mr Hickok would want you to have the wire.' The young man handed the telegraph message to Dix and scratched his head. He could not have been more than twenty-five, yet he was already losing his hair. 'What kinda things could a man catch off these females, sir?'

'Bad things.' Dan touched the side of his nose and winked.

The man shrugged. He was none the wiser.

'I'd best get back to the office.'

Dix touched the brim of his hat and watched as the young man strolled across the sawdust-covered floor back to the swing-doors. He pushed them open and then lingered for a few seconds as if trying to work out what the ranchers had meant. Then he strolled out into the darkness.

'What's it say, Dixie?' Dan asked. He straightened up in his chair and rested his elbows on the green baize.

Dix looked at the neatly folded paper.

'You were a lawman for most of your life, Dan. Right?'

'Right.'

'OK,' Dix continued. 'I thought it was against the law to read another man's mail?'

Dan rubbed the corners of his mouth.

'Does that include wires, Dixie?'

Dix smiled and pointed at the landing.

'It don't matter none now anyways. Wild Bill seems to have finished his business upstairs.'

Dan Shaw turned his head and looked up at the open door directly opposite them. The unmistakable figure of Hickok walked out on to the landing and then closed the door behind him. He put his frock-coat back on as he descended the staircase towards the saloon floor.

'You got a reply to your wire, Bill,' Dan said.

Hickok pushed his long hair off his face, grabbed a bottle off the bar, then made his way slowly towards the card-table.

'Read it,' he ordered.

'We thought you'd want to read it yourself,' Dan said.

Hickok turned a chair around backwards and sat on it. He placed the bottle down on the table, sighed heavily and rubbed his hooded eyes with the palms of his hands.

'My eyes don't like reading lately, boys,' he confessed. 'I figure the ink is getting greyer nowadays. You read it.'

Tom Dix unfolded the paper. 'I'll read it for you.'

Hickok nodded and picked up the bottle. He placed the black glass to his mouth and swallowed at least five fingers of rotgut whiskey. He returned the bottle to the table and rested his brow on his wrists.

'You're a good man, Dixie.'

Dix started to read.

'It says: "Wild Bill, you must have been reading my mind. I do need new blood for my herd. I'll pay eight hundred dollars for a pedigree white-face bull. Tell your pals to bring it to my ranch at San Remo. Best, Kirby".'

Hickok nodded and looked up at his two friends.

'I told you that he'd come up trumps for us, boys.'

'Where's his ranch?' Dan asked.

'Where's San Remo?' Dix added.

'The Double B.' Hickok said. His long fingers drew a thin cigar from his pocket and placed it between his teeth. 'It's on the Californian coast, I'm told.'

'California?' Dan Shaw gasped. 'How are we gonna get our bull to California?'

Wild Bill struck a match and put its flame just below the tip of his cigar. He inhaled deeply and smiled.

'By train!'

'There ain't no trains that go all the way to the California coast, Bill,' Shaw said. 'Hell! I ain't sure if they go to California either.'

'They do now, Dan. The Union Pacific just finished laying its tracks from here to San Francisco,' Hickok informed his pals. 'That's got to be fate, boys. Pure and simple fate.'

Dix leaned forward.

'From Cheyenne to 'Frisco?'

'Yep.' The gunfighter took another swig from the whiskey-bottle. 'That's why them stock-pens are full of steers, Dixie. The cattle-owners heard that the railroad company was opening the new line out of Cheyenne to San Francisco. That's a whole new market for beef on the hoof. We take the train with our horses and your bull. From 'Frisco we head south. San Remo is on the coast someplace. We'll find it.'

'We?' Dan pushed the brim of his hat off his brow and looked at the tired gunfighter. 'Did I hear right?'

'You heard right, Dan,' Hickok answered.

'You coming with us, James Butler?' Dix asked. 'All the way to California?'

Hickok tapped his cigar ash on to the floor and nodded.

'Sure thing, Dixie. Someone's gotta show you boys the way to my old pal Kirby Jones's spread.'

Dixie grinned.

'It wouldn't happen to have anything to do with the ruckus we had with them cowpokes earlier, would it? That fat marshal might try his hand at arresting you again.'

Hickok placed the cigar back in his mouth.

'Yep, reckon it might get a tad warm around here when that fat fool wakes up again. How long do you figure it'll take you boys to go and get that bull?'

'About ten minutes.' Dix smiled. 'We got him down at Parker's Livery.'

Hickok looked up at the wall clock and squinted.

'The train to California is due out at eight.'

'With any luck we'll be headed to California

43

before the marshal wakes up.' Dan smiled.

'That gives us plenty of time to get our bull and horses down to them railroad tracks.' Dixie nodded.

All three men's attention was drawn to a black bat as it swooped in over the swing-doors and chased a moth across the well-illuminated saloon.

Automatically, Hickok drew one of his guns, cocked its hammer and fired. The bat was hit dead centre. It fell limply into the sawdust at his feet.

He stared at it for a while before looking up at his companions.

'C'mon, boys.' he said holstering his smoking Colt. 'Let's get out of here before this flying mouse's kinfolk show up and start trouble.'

All three rose and headed out into the street.

FIVE

The westward-bound train had pulled out ten minutes ahead of schedule on its long journey to the Pacific Ocean and the sprawling city of San Franciso, which had earned its dubious reputation the hard way. The powerful locomotive had a hard trip ahead of it. It had to negotiate not only the awesome Rockies, but also the equally foreboding Sierras. Plumes of choking black smoke had billowed out of its tall chimney up into the blue morning sky and hung on the crisp cold air.

It was still there when trail boss Byron Harding whipped his lathered-up stallion furiously ahead of a dozen or more of his cowboys through the streets of Cheyenne towards the hundreds of stock-pens near the gleaming tracks. He reined in, leapt from his saddle and mounted the steps of the railroad building two at a time.

He kicked the door open and glared at the startled faces of the men inside. There were more than a dozen people within the large area. A wall of small glass panes gave a view of the gleaming tracks below. A line of points levers ran the entire length of the wall opposite Harding. A man with a rag in his hands moved along the levers, pulling some back and others forward as trains were shunted on to the correct tracks. Another man was dressed in an expensive suit with a golden watch-chain hanging across his vest-front. The rest seemed to be simply clerks who carried papers from one place to another.

Harding's eyes were burning like hot coals as he studied the clerks. Then he returned his attention to the man in the well-tailored suit. The trail boss pushed chairs and desks aside and headed straight for him.

The startled man instinctively made to flee.

Harding was too fast for him. The cowboy had carved a path through the obstacles right up to the terrified man until he was cornered.

'W . . . what do you want?' the startled figure stuttered.

'I want Hickok!' Harding screamed as both his fists came down on the top of the desk. Papers went cascading in every direction. 'Where's Hickok?'

The man staggered back and fell into his well-padded leather chair. He grabbed a sheet of paper and fanned himself as he stared into the unblinking eyes of the trail boss.

'Hickok? You mean Wild Bill Hickok?'

'You know anyone else named Hickok, mister?' Harding picked up a letter-opener and rammed its blade down into the ink blotter.

'I . . . I guess there's only one Hickok,' the man stammered.

'You seen him?' Harding growled.

'Yes, sir.' The man nodded. 'He was here about six with two other men. They hired a stock-car for their animals. A bull and three horses.'

Harding moved to the wall of glass and stared down at the railtracks and cattle-pens below.

'Is he still here?'

'No. He and his friends left.'

'Where'd they go?'

'They left on the eight o'clock train to California.'

Byron Harding swung around and glared at the seated man. He strode up to him and leaned over the terrified creature. 'They took a train?'

The man nodded.

'Yes.'

'How far they going on it?' Harding drew his gun and cocked its hammer.

'All the way to San Francisco.'

Harding's expression altered. Suddenly he was no longer looking angry. Now he was looking confused. He moved closer to the shaking railroad boss with the gun in his gloved hand.

'How many stops are there between here and there?'

'At least thirty. Mostly for taking on water. Some are towns that folks live in.' The man pointed to a detailed map on the wall behind him. 'They're all marked up there on the map. But why do you ask?'

'I want to catch Hickok!' Harding snapped.

'But why?'

' 'Coz he killed a dozen of my Triple Bar cowboys last night!' The cowboy stared down at the floor. 'We just come from the funeral parlour. My boys are stacked up in there like planks of lumber. Me and the rest of my outfit was camped just outside town and got curious why half my boys didn't ride back to camp this morning.'

'I'd not go up against Hickok, friend,' the rail-road boss advised. 'He's a gunfighter.'

'I ain't always bin a cowboy!' Harding spat. 'I know how to use my hogleg!'

'But he's with two other men. I think that they're gunfighters as well.'

'It don't matter none!'

'But the train is long gone!'

Harding's eyes narrowed. He walked up to the large map and studied it. It showed the entire rail-road system in perfect detail.

'Is this map up to date, *amigo*?'

'It's brand-new, sir. We only started the California route a month or so back. They sent that map from back East.'

Harding released the hammer on his gun and slid it back into his weathered holster. He pulled a penknife from his pants pocket and opened up its blade.

'What are you going to do?' The alarmed man in the comfortable chair squealed as sunlight flashed across the honed blade.

Byron Harding slid the blade around the edge of the map, cut it from its wooden frame, then rolled it up neatly.

'That's railroad property,' the man said.

Harding pulled a silver dollar from his leather vest-pocket and tossed it into the lap of the railroad boss.

'Buy another one!' he shouted as he kicked the table over and marched back out into the morning air. He jumped down to the dusty ground and took his reins off one of his cowboys. 'I got me a map, boys!'

A wrangler called Vance steadied his buckskin quarter horse and tossed the remnants of a cigarette away.

'Where's Hickok, boss?' he asked.

'Running away on a train, Vance!'

'Ya mean we lost the critter?'

'Lost him? I don't think so!' Harding unrolled the map and stared at it carefully. A smile etched its way across his weathered features as he ran a thumbnail over the surface before jabbing it almost through the paper. 'That train has gotta go right around that bunch of mountains before it reaches its first watering-stop. It takes time to do that. We can take a short cut by riding through Dry Gulch. We'll be there a long time before that trains shows up.'

The cowboys all grunted in agreement.

'You gonna tangle square-on with Wild Bill, boss?' Vance asked as he watched the trail boss roll the map up again. 'He's a cold blooded killer that don't give an inch.'

'I've faced better, Vance!' Harding boasted.

'Ya have?'

The trail boss plucked a silver button from his vest and tossed it high into the air. With the speed of a gunslinger, he drew and fired. The button was hit and flew off over the roof of the railroad building.

The cowboys gasped in amazement as he holstered his smoking Colt.

'I can do that with either hand,' he said.

'Then how come ya only got one gun, boss?' Vance queried.

' 'Coz when you're as good as me with a six-shooter, you only need one gun, boy!' Harding threw himself on to the back of his stallion, poked his boots into his stirrups and turned the horse around to face his men. 'Hickok's gonna pay for killing Triple Bar cowboys! He's gonna pay with his life!'

The horsemen spurred hard and rode in the direction of Dry Gulch.

SIX

It was a natural harbour, deep and well-sheltered. Its small cove was only accessible from the sea. Tree-covered cliffs towered over the array of well-disguised buildings which nestled on stilts above the clear water against the highest of tides. At low tide a beach of yellow sand traced along the base of the almost vertical green cliff-face. The harbour was large enough for three wooden gunboats to rest at anchor without ever being spotted from outside the cove. Yet only one such vessel had ever entered this secret place.

This was a sanctuary known to only those who used it. Since it had first been discovered by accident, only a few more than a hundred men had entered Dead Man's Rest. Just over twelve months later there were fewer than half that amount left alive, for these men had eventful yet short existences. They dealt in death and paid a high price for mistakes.

Without the shelter of Dead Man's Rest they all

knew that they too would have joined their dead shipmates in Davy Jones's locker by now. For there were few places close to the long coastline which offered any protection for their breed. A few hundred miles north of their secret cove, the prosperous San Francisco bathed in a mixture of barbaric civilization. Bankers rubbed shoulders with the lowliest of creatures and yet there was no welcome for these men even in the meanest of San Francisco's gutters.

The cove was less than forty miles north of the small coastal port of San Remo. Yet the seas south of there were still a mystery to them.

Dead Man's Cove served its new masters well. It gave them shelter from the hazardous winds which swept along the coast, and also from the prying eyes of those who sought out the deadly sea-dogs whom it protected.

No navy cutter, however fast and agile, had even realized what lay within their own backyard. For Dead Man's Rest did not even exist on the most detailed of admiralty maps. From the sea, there was no hint of anything but a straight uninterrupted coastline.

Yet it did exist and so did the magnificent ship and men who crewed it.

No one knew the exact origins of either the sleek twin-masted vessel or the men who sailed upon her tar-sealed decks beneath the flowing black canvas sails. But it was the black flag with its simple white-painted skull at it centre which told the story to any who managed to survive a bloody, unwanted encounter.

Few ever lived to tell tales, though.

Those who had managed to survive were usually considered to have lost their grip on sanity.

For this was a ship and a crew which harked back to a time more than a century before. A time when pirates were rife and haunted the slow Spanish galleons. Most thought that the rogues of the high seas had vanished for ever, yet the pirates never truly disappeared. Most simply sailed to less dangerous seas where the pickings were just as great as they had once been in the Caribbean.

The pirates knew that there was a world to plunder far beyond the Caribbean and few were willing or able to prevent it happening.

They had sailed to the four corners of the globe on the scent of gold, ivory and precious gems. Generations later their descendants and an army of eager new recruits continued to ply their evil and ancient trade. It seemed that no matter how many pirates died, there was always more than enough new blood ready to replace them.

After more than three decades the news of the discovery of gold in California had reached even the most remote regions of the globe. It came to the ears of men who existed only by their greed and deadly skills.

Gold was an irresistible lure which had cursed

men for centuries. A bait that tempted even honest souls. Thirty years had not seemed to dim the flame of lust for the yellow ore in the hearts of the countless thousands who had travelled to the Golden State. They had come from all over the world in search of their own personal bonanza. For nearly all of them, it had been a vain quest.

Of all the pirate ships, only one had successfully made the hazardous journey across the vast ocean to its goal. It had filled its mighty sails with the unseen wind and navigated its way between a thousand islands before reaching the long notorious coastline.

Finding Dead Man's Rest during a savage storm shortly after their arrival had proved to be the salvation of the pirates. They hastily constructed their buildings and a place where they could beach the long ship for repairs. Barnacles did not respect even the most deadly of ship hulls and had to be dealt with on a regular basis.

For more than a year one apparent accident after another befell the merchant ships which travelled through the Californian waters. Ships disappeared, as did their cargoes and crew. With few survivors of any merit, no one even suspected what had really occurred.

It seemed impossible even to contemplate.

So it continued unchecked.

The ship came out of the mist fast. Like a

dolphin in full aquatic flight. White water spray arched off its bow to both sides of the black, gleaming, wooden bulkheads. It glistened in the haunting light of the large, pale-yellow moon. Under full sail, it simply could not be bettered for speed. This was a heavily gunned boat like no other. A vessel that was in a class of its own. A high-bred wooden creation which seemed to be almost alive, as some rare inanimate objects often do.

Somehow it had become more than just another twin-master.

After the heat of battle, its wounds had been patched and sealed with tar more times than any of its crew could recall. Yet each time it was repaired, it seemed to become better than it had been before.

Faster than the wind itself, it was said.

Could it have become a living entity as those who crewed it swore? Had the lives and deaths of those who served her like faithful slaves made this long narrow creation something more than just another boat?

Sanity said it could never be so.

Yet few sane men ever ventured from the safety of land to the dangers of the deep oceans. For there a man was at the mercy of something far more dangerous than mere gods. At sea, there was only one mistress.

And she was far more cruel than even the most fearful of gods. The sea could be a generous benefactor and yet her mood could change faster than the most irrational of creatures. She would seek revenge on those who did not respect and worship her.

Of all the ships that dared to challenge the might of the sea, none did it better than the *Black Serpent*.

Whatever type of vessel the ship had originally been, that had been long ago. She had been altered and modified beyond recognition during her years in the Orient. Only the two tall masts remained the same. Even the sails and rigging had been totally changed in a constant attempt to find the perfect setting to catch every last breath of wind.

Now the wooden ship was something it had never been before its transformation. It was a killing machine. Even with its score of cannon, it was still fast. Faster than anything else on the high seas.

Twenty cannons flanked both port and starboard sides of the long, slender ship. With every ounce of spare weight removed, the *Black Serpent*'s perfect balance meant it could not be matched for speed.

The *Black Serpent* did not merely sail as other ships sailed through the blue waters. It sliced like a cutlass through them. It was more than just a ship. It was a missile. It had no equal, and its crew and captain knew it.

The forty-year-old captain had long ago been an outlaw to match any in the West, yet that had been before he had found a more lucrative career. As Tall Red, he had discovered his true vocation. At almost six foot two inches tall, with a scarlet mane of hair and a beard to match, he was a fearful sight. Tall Red had the ruthlessness to match his appearance. He had killed the last captain of the *Black Serpent* a few years earlier for no better reason than that he wanted the ship for himself. None of the rest of the crew voiced any objections.

They did not want to die so pointlessly.

These were men who were called pirates but in reality most were just bandits who had somehow found themselves shipboard with like-minded vermin. Bandits who plied their ruthless trade on sea as well as land with equal precision. Men who sought, found and ultimately plundered the treasures others had toiled for.

A dozen countries had spawned these evil bloodthirsty men and they had no betters at controlling the long, slender ship, or killing those who stood in their way.

They had moulded themselves from being dangerous individuals into one fearsome and merciless animal. Unlike bandits who remained on the land, they had never found themselves cornered by the law. There were no box canyons where they roamed. Just waves that went on for ever.

Their only real enemy was ignorance. The knowledge of a new sea took time to learn and chart. Sailing into new waters always held dangers. Unseen whirlpools, coral reefs and underwater rocks all had the ability to wreck even the best-armoured of vessels.

Yet they were not fearful. Only wary.

Nothing frightened these demons in human form. They worshipped only the plunder that they took. No gods found their way into these heartless souls. They lived for the present, knowing that at any time the powerful sea could snatch them as it had snatched countless others who had dared challenge its supremacy over the centuries.

Life is said to have begun in the sea. These men knew it could also end there.

As with all men who spend most of their time at sea, they were superstitious. Tattoos to prevent them drowning were known not to work, and yet each of them had succumbed to the ink and needle. They were all convinced that the sea was their mistress and had many secrets hidden in the depths where no man would ever be able to swim. The black depths were where monstrous creatures known as serpents lived in underwater canyons which it was said could be more than five miles deep. The seamen knew that without warning these monsters could break surface, strike and crush even the sturdiest ship in half as if it were the driest of kindling. Then a mere heartbeat later, they would disappear.

Serpents of the sea had been mythical legends since time had started. But all myths have some foundation in truth. The most learned of men in their marble museums had said that such things did not exist, but were the imaginings of rum-soaked minds. But none of them had ever sailed where these men dared to sail. They had not tasted the brine in their mouths.

Whatever the truth, only the sea knew all the answers and she would never tell mere humans.

She who tolerated their presence. She who had the ability to drag them down to untold depths until their lungs shrank to the size of dried peas before their bodies exploded to feed the schools of fish that always trailed ships wherever they sailed.

Each of the hardened cut-throats knew they could never afford to lose their respect for her. She was the one thing that they had no control over. They were forever at her mercy.

That superstition was their only weakness.

The *Black Serpent* moved speedily through the night waters like a hungry panther on the scent of its next conquest. She had been seeking prey to satisfy her insatiable appetite for hours since leaving the safety of Dead Man's Rest. Captain and crew were fired-up with hard liquor and ready for action. They would not return to their safe harbour until they had achieved their goal. The *Black Serpent* used the fog which rolled over the dark water to her advantage as she searched for a fresh kill. Then a cry came down from the crow's nest.

'Ship ahoy, Captain!' an eagle-eyed pirate called down to the quarter deck filled with well armed men. 'Port bow!'

SEVEN

Only the light of the large yellow moon illuminated the *Black Serpent* as she cut through the fog and steadily reduced the distance between herself and her unwary prey. The hull of the long vessel rose up and down on the rolling waves with the grace of an antelope. Her black sails were swollen as the helmsman kept his charge on course to intercept the far larger Navy gunboat. The *Black Serpent* rode the waves like a cowboy breaking a mustang. Defiant of the violent movement beneath his boot-leather, Tall Red strode steadily across the deck until he was beside the port rail. He gritted his teeth, raised his telescope to his left eye and adjusted the focus carefully until he could see through the moonlit fog at the Navy cutter.

'That ain't no merchant ship!' he growled angrily. 'Damn it all!'

'I reckon we ought to leave it, Tall Red,' said a short, round creature called Skin. Skin had tattoos covering almost every inch of his body including his face. He rested both hands on the rail. 'Ain't no profit on them Navy boats.'

Tall Red nodded in partial agreement.

'Wait up. Ain't that the same damn boat that's bin dogging us for the past couple of weeks, Skin?'

The shorter man accepted the telescope and stared through the mist until he could get a bead on the Naval warship.

'You mean the one that took a couple of shots at us last month when we was closing in on that Frenchie three-master? Sure looks like her. Why?'

'I don't like being dogged by no sailor boys!' Tall Red replied. 'Especially one that makes us lose our prize. Reminds me of the posses that used to hunt my hide back when I was a young outlaw. You can't let them creep up on you. Nope, that ship is starting to get troublesome. So far we've been lucky, but there's only one way to stop them for good.'

'But why risk it, Tall Red?' Skin asked as the long sleek boat forged a course in the larger vessel's wake. 'We was looking for an old merchant. Something full of vittles for us to take back to Dead Man's Rest. Why take *her* on?'

Tall Red slapped the back of the smaller man.

' 'Coz I like a good fight, Skin. Besides, it's only a matter of time before they get themselves a good look at us and then we'll have us a whole herd of Navy boats hunting us. Anyway, Ching Ho and his boys need a bit of target practice.'

Skin knew the captain had made up his mind and there was no point arguing with him. Not unless you relished being thrown to the sharks.

'We going to sink her, Tall Red?'

'After we get what we want from their holds.'

'You figure that they got fresh provisions and grog aboard, Tall Red?' the tattooed man asked as the rest of the crew manned their posts.

'Sure enough. They're just out of 'Frisco, ain't they?' Tall Red sneered as his eyes burned at the ship ahead of them. 'They got to have fresh vittles and liquor aboard. We're going to take it off them and anything else they got in their holds, Skin!'

Skin tucked the telescope under his arm and rubbed his hands together eagerly. He drooled at the thought of sinking what teeth he had left into food that had yet to be infested by worm.

'They might have salted bacon aboard, Captain. I sure do like my bacon. And eggs. They might have real eggs.'

Tall Red walked to the top of the port stairwell and cupped his hands to either side of his bearded mouth. He filled his lungs and bellowed.

'Ching Ho! Get your sorry hide up here!'

'I come, Captain!' A pale yellow-skinned man appeared from out of the crowd of shiphands on the well deck. He had mere slits for eyes and a long plaited pigtail which hung down to his belt. He ran up the wooden steps until he was beside Tall Red.

Tall Red grabbed his cannon master's shoulder and dragged him close until his bearded mouth was next to the man's ringed ear.

'Does Ching Ho want to do some target practice?'

The face of the Chinese pirate lit up.

'What you want Ching Ho to aim cannons at, Tall Red?'

'See that boat over yonder?' The captain pointed at the heavily armed Naval gunboat. 'You want to blow the masts off that fat old cutter?'

Ching Ho nodded but looked disappointed.

'No money on that ship I bet you. You joke with Ching Ho maybe?'

'Tall Red don't joke with nobody,' the captain growled. 'I'm asking you if you can cut them masts off at deck-height? Can you do it?'

'Easy!' Ching Ho nodded. 'But no profit in attacking Navy boats. They got no gold.'

'Get some cannons trained on them,' Tall Red said. 'I want you to blast every scrap of rigging off that elephant and then see how many of its cannons you can hit.'

'We not sink her?'

'Eventually, Ching Ho! Eventually! First we got to cripple her and then see what they got in her hold. We needs us a lot of provisions and I'm betting they got some damn fresh grub stowed below decks. Them fancy officers eat real well, I'm told.'

'Then do we sink her?'

'Yep. Then we sink her,' Tall Red confirmed.

'Good. No like Navy boats.'

'How long before you can prime and fire them port cannons, Ching Ho?' Tall Red asked as men started to climb up the rigging toward the sails.

'Ten minutes maybe!'

Tall Red grinned and patted the Chinaman on his head.

'Make it five minutes and you got yourself a whole barrel of rum to share with your boys. OK?'

'OK!' Ching Ho chuckled and slid along the hand-rail back down to the lower deck. He frantically started to muster his well-trained men around their cannons. The Oriental had no equal when it came to handling anything to do with gunpowder. It was said that he had once been a slave to one of China's most powerful mandarins. A man who liked fireworks and explosions. Ching Ho had provided both before blowing up the highly paid Chinese civil servant and fleeing.

Like a well-oiled machine, the men packed the barrels of the cannons with powder, wadding and ball before ramming all three down with their long poles. Ching Ho marched up and down his port-side crew, adjusting the heavy weapons before he placed small fuses in the holes at the rear of the cannons. A powder-horn sprinkled the black granules around each of the fuses in turn. Ching Ho then lit a well-tarred torch and held it above his head as his narrow eyes studied his men's progress.

He would wait until every one of them raised their right hands to signal they were ready before moving along the line of primed cannons.

But he would not lower the flame on to the fuses until Tall Red gave the order.

Only then would he act.

Skin closed the telescope and returned it to his smiling captain.

'They got a lot more cannon on that old boat than we have, Tall Red. More than twice as many.'

'But their gun crew are sleeping, Skin!'

'I'm still a tad worried!'

Tall Red laughed. He grabbed hold of the rigging and jumped up on to the wet rail.

'Just think of all that juicy bacon, Skin. And them eggs.'

There was no audible reply from the tattooed man. Just a toothless smile.

Tall Red pointed to the stocky crewman at the helm. It was a signal that required no words.

The helmsman spun the wheel. The long, slender boat lurched to port and began to close the distance between the *Black Serpent* and its unsuspecting target.

'Get your weapons ready, boys!' the captain called out to the rest of his men below him. 'Soon the sea will be red! Blood-red!'

Ten gunners' arms were raised. Ching Ho waved the flaming torch to his captain and waited.

*

The skeleton crew aboard the large USS *Robert Armstrong* had never seen action. The boat had only been in Californian waters for six weeks, after a long perilous journey around the Horn. It had left the shipyards of New York after being refitted and would be permanently based in the bays of San Francisco.

Dozens of oil-lanterns swayed along the length of the magnificent ship as the heavy gunboat ploughed slowly on its course back to its new home port. Unlike the hunter that stalked her, she was bathed in light. The half-dozen sailors who manned her decks were more asleep than awake. Only the helmsman remained alert, but his eyes were aimed directly ahead at the bow.

The *Black Serpent* suddenly came through the swirling mist. It drew alongside the larger vessel. Less than twenty yards of ocean separated them.

The sailor on the wheel of the *Robert Armstrong* looked round in a mixture of shock and total horror. His eyes narrowed and focused on the figure that clung to the rigging. The wind and spray blew the long hair and beard of Tall Red as the *Black Serpent*'s captain looked down at Ching Ho with his blazing torch held in his hands.

'Fire!' Tall Red screamed out over and over.

Ching Ho ran down the line of primed cannons. His flaming torch touched the black powder and ignited each of the fuses in turn. Less than a second separated the cannons' firing. Plumes of smoke billowed before deadly iron balls flew across the distance between the ships.

As always, the aim of the gunners was true. The towering masts shattered at deck-level, bringing their sails and rigging crashing down.

Before the sleeping crew knew what was happening above them, the *Black Serpent* had sailed alongside the *Robert Armstrong*. Its heavily armed pirates expertly lashed both vessels together before boarding their helpless victim.

Like an army of soldier ants the pirates swarmed up and over the Navy gunboat's bulkheads. The handful of sailors on night watch offered little resistance to the guns and knives of Tall Red's bloodthirsty crew.

It took only minutes for Tall Red's lethal confederates to get below decks and locate the rest of the *Robert Armstrong*'s sailors.

Before sinking the larger ship, the pirates maimed and killed each of the stunned half-asleep sailors. They showed no mercy. No compassion. Whether their victims were able-bodied, wounded or even asleep, the fate of each was the same.

Only after they had plundered every scrap of food, water and hard drink to be found in the ship's galley and holds did they set their victim loose.

As the vessels drifted apart, Ching Ho's cannons

blasted oil-soaked wads of burning material into the heart of their helpless foe.

A few moments before the summer sun rose out of the distant watery horizon, Tall Red's words came true.

Flames engulfed the wooden hulk.

The sea did turn red.

Blood-red.

EIGHT

A million stars sparkled like precious jewels above the dusty prairie as the Triple Bar horsemen made their way through the hot, arid canyon towards the moonlit water-tower. Byron Harding had been right about reaching this remote railroad place before the massive locomotive had come round the unnamed mountain. He and his thirteen cowboys had hauled rein just as the sun disappeared below the top of the jagged skyline. They had been riding for nearly seven hours without stop to reach this place before the train. They had endured the blistering heat of the merciless sun until the skin was almost burned from their faces, yet not one of them had slowed his pace. Each of the cowboys had the same burning desire eating at his innards. They wanted revenge at any cost.

Nothing else would satisfy them.

Hickok had to pay for what he had done.

Harding, unlike his trail crew, knew that men like Wild Bill were no easy targets. They had lived life on both sides of the law and only remained alive because they were good at what they did.

And what they did was kill.

They could unleash their lethal venom without warning at the first sign of trouble. To underestimate men of Hickok's calibre was to sign your own death certificate.

The trail boss dismounted and studied the barren outpost carefully. He knew that if he were to make good his words of getting even with the legendary Wild Bill Hickok, he would have to ensure that the stage was set to his advantage.

It was true that Harding had not always been a man who earned his keep taking herds from Texas to the railhead towns of Kansas and beyond. There had been a time when the name of Byron Harding had almost equalled that of Hickok himself.

But Harding had chosen a less complicated existence. He had never had a taste for hard liquor or the skill to frequent gaming-tables. Loose women were also something he simply had little or no time for. He had found his own true happiness on the cattle ranges where he had raised a large family.

He saw fame for what it really was. A fleeting and often worthless weight to hang around the necks of those who took their own existence too seriously. He had seen many great gunfighters backshot by worthless creatures with no skill except that of taking advantage of someone's lapse of concentration.

Byron Harding had known that his days were numbered if he remained a man who hired out his gun to others. For there is always someone younger. Someone faster. Someone more hungry for success.

Perhaps if he had met Ned Buntline, like Hickok, Wyatt Earp and Buffalo Bill, and had had his life exaggerated beyond all reason, he too might have become another living legend. But Harding had never been a colourful creature with flamboyant attire. He had never adopted the gaudy garb of so many men of his profession.

He was just rugged.

His gunfighting skills had been his only vice. It had been one he had learned to control before it had destroyed him. He had seen how so many other hired guns had simply gone on far too long. He had never wanted the reputation he had earned all those years earlier.

Byron Harding had been smarter than most of his rare breed; had simply quit to live a real life in hopes of reaching a reasonable age before meeting the Grim Reaper.

Yet the slaughter of so many of his cowboys had stirred up something within him that he had thought dead and buried. The demons had returned to his soul and they were once again urging him to kill

He tied his stallion to a weathered tree and stared up at the high water-tower. Water dripped at regular intervals on to the ground at its base. Even in the eerie light of the stars and moon, a few green weeds could be seen flourishing amid a waste of sand.

'Water the horses, boys!' Harding drawled in the Texan accent he had acquired over the previous decades. 'And make sure they're out of the line of fire!'

'OK, boss!' one of the cowboys piped up.

The rest of the cowboys tied their mounts to trees and brush before moving to the sides of the thoughtful man who stood looking along the gleaming railtracks.

'What we gonna do if Hickok and his buddies get off the train to face you, boss?' Vance asked as he rolled a cigarette, his tobacco-pouch hanging from one of his teeth.

Harding glaced around his men. They were all hardened by years of eating dust on countless trail drives. Every one of them was loyal and honest. Yet not one of them had an inkling of what it meant to face up to another man in a showdown.

Especially a man like Wild Bill Hickok.

Even in their most horrific nightmares they had never sensed what it was like to lay your life on the line and try to outdraw another. To risk everything on the belief that you were the fastest draw alive. A score of faces burned into the memory of the trail boss. Faces of men he had sent to their Maker.

Faces he had thought were long forgotten.

'You boys gotta stay out of this, you hear?' Harding snapped, resting a boot on one of the gleaming rail tracks.

'But why?' Vance asked.

' 'Coz Wild Bill Hickok will make widows of your wives just like he did with the rest of our outfit,' the trail boss explained. 'I go up against him alone. Only me! Savvy?'

The cowboys began to move closer.

'That ain't fair, boss,' a cowboy named Toby moaned. 'We all want to kill that critter and his pals.'

'Toby's right!' Vance snorted. He struck a match and lit his cigarette. 'We got blistered backsides riding here with you all day. The least ya can do is let us join in the fun.'

'Fun?' Harding's head turned and stared at the man with smoke drifting from his mouth. 'You think facing someone like Hickok is fun? How old are you, Vance?'

'I'm nearly twenty-something,' Vance answered coyly.

'And still wet behind the ears!' Harding growled.

'That ain't no may to talk to us, boss.' Toby exhaled.

Harding drew his gun, quickly checked it, then slid it back into its holster.

'Those cowboys that Hickok slaughtered were

Triple Bar men and I've a duty to try and bring him to book.'

'On ya own?'

'Hickok is deadly.' Harding spoke from experience. 'I knew him twenty years back. That man is mean. He'll kill someone who just looks at him the wrong way. Kinda crazy in the head from all the infected females he's bedded. They reckon he's got the fever eating at his brain. But he's still one of the best gunfighters who ever lived and breathed. If I don't outdraw the critter, I'm dead. If you boys try to help me, you'll all be dead as well. Savvy?'

'I'm willing to back you up, boss,' Vance said. He pulled the cigarette from his mouth, dropped it on to the sand and crushed it under his boot.

'We all are, boss!' another of the cowboys piped up.

Reluctantly Harding nodded.

'OK! I tried to warn you!'

The cowboys' smiles could be seen in the haunting light.

'Wild Bill's in for a surprise!' Vance chuckled.

Suddenly, Byron Harding looked down at the boot he had resting on the gleaming rail. His eyes narrowed as he raised his head and stared at his trail crew.

'The train's coming, boys!'

'How'd ya know?' Toby asked. 'I can't hear nothing.'

Harding pointed at his boot.

'I can feel the vibration on the track.'

The cowboys fell silent as Harding took two steps forward and stared off into the distance.

'Take cover, boys,' he said. 'She's coming!'

NINE

Like ominous signals from an Indian fire, plumes of smoke rose up into the darkness as the massive locomotive exercised its metal might and moved steadily up the steep gradient towards the water-tower. Red sparks floated towards the distant heavens as the cattle-guard of the locomotive came slowly into view. Moonlight glanced along the gleaming surface of the train's powerful body lighting up the jets of white hot steam that spat out from beside its wheels.

The sound of metal grating on metal filled the surrounding area as the brakes were gently applied. The engineer and his stoker leaned out from the cab and stared up the tracks at the blazing torch. It had been rammed in the ground right in the middle of the wooden sleepers. Its blood-red flame danced in the gentle night air.

'What in tarnation is going on?' the engineer said, keeping his gloved hand on the throttle of his mighty charge.

'Might be train robbers!' the stoker suggested.

The engineer rubbed the sweat off his face.

'Don't matter who it is, Jacob. We gotta stop to take on water for the boiler. This old girl won't get to the next stop without a bellyful of water.'

The cowboys rested their backs against the rugged rocks beside the water-tower and watched as the train laboured its way closer to their hiding-places. Each of the trail-weary riders watched Harding.

They would do nothing until he did.

As the train stopped a few feet from the torch, the cowboys walked out into the light of the loco-motive's lantern and stood defiantly across the track.

Like a man possessed of hidden demons, Harding moved away from his men until he was directly below the high engineer's cab and the two confused men. His right hand rested on the grip of his gun as he squinted up at the engineer and his companion.

'Is this a hold-up?' the engineer asked.

'Don't fret none! You can go about your busi-ness,' Harding stated. 'I'm here for only one reason and that's bringing Hickok to heel! I ain't got truck with you.'

The engineer leaned further down.

'You figurin' on taking on Wild Bill?' he gasped.

'Damn right!' Harding snorted angrily.

'Are ya loco? He just left a whole heap of dead

men back at Cheyenne, boy,' the man stated. 'Get out of here before he does the same to you. He's bad news!'

'I know damn well he left a heap of dead bodies back in Cheyenne,' the trail boss snarled. They were my boys. Hickok killed half my cowboys! That's why I'm here! He's gonna pay!'

'Hickok's got fire in his eyes, mister!' the stoker warned. 'He'll kill ya for sure. He's got the taste. Men like him are dangerous when they got the taste of blood in their mouths!'

Byron Harding was not easily frightened or dissuaded.

'Where is he?'

The stoker wiped his hands with a greasy rag, then looked back at the line of cars strung out behind the wood-filled tender. He pointed.

'The first car. But be careful. He ain't alone.'

'I heard tell he's travelling with two other men. Is that right?'

The engineer nodded first.

'Yep. Rough characters. One looks like he's a gunslinger or worse. Got himself a pair of matched Colts in the fanciest shooting-rig I ever done set eyes upon. Watch out for him. The other one is nothin' special.'

'He got a name? The man with the guns?' Harding pressed. His eyes darted from the well-lit car to the men above him.

A voice came out of the shadows.

'Tom Dix! His name's Tom Dix!'

Harding turned swiftly and drew his gun faster than the blink of an eye. He had cocked its hammer even before the barrel of the trusty weapon had cleared its holster.

'Who's there?' he snapped as he trained the gun into the shadows. 'Show yourself!'

The train's conductor walked towards the cowboy and stared at the deadly Colt. He seemed unimpressed.

'You're a tad nervous there, stranger!' he noted. 'I'd not take on Hickok or Dix in your condition. Those boys got nerves of steel, I'm told!'

Harding started to breath again.

'Did you say Tom Dix?'

'That's what I said.' the conductor confirmed. 'You know of him? He's a rancher!'

Harding lowered the gun.

'He might be a rancher now but there was a time when he was one of the highest-paid gunfighters in Texas,' he said. 'I thought he was dead.'

The conductor raised an eyebrow. 'Nope, he ain't dead. He's seen better days, but he sure ain't dead. I'd not want to cross him. He sure seems to be pally with Hickok.'

'Who's the other man with Wild Bill?' Harding asked.

'Name of Shaw. Dan Shaw.'

Harding looked troubled.

'Never heard of him.'

'He's a retired US marshal,' the conductor answered. 'Wild Bill is in pretty choice company and no mistake. I'd think twice about taking him on. Even if you won the fight you might find yourself hanging from a tree-branch.'

Harding narrowed his eyes.

'They ain't made the rope that'll hang me, old-timer. Just go and tell Wild Bill that Byron Harding wants him out here!'

The conductor licked his dry lips.

'Are you sure?'

'Damn right I'm sure!' Harding growled.

'You looking for me, Byron?' The familiar voice drifted on the gentle breeze.

Harding recognized the voice. A cold shiver traced up his spine. He tilted his head and stared along the car at the tall, long-haired figure as he stepped down from the first car on to the dusty ground.

There was no mistaking Hickok.

Even in the shadows, it was impossible to confuse him with any other living creature.

'Yep, I'm looking for you, Wild Bill! We got a score to settle!' Harding shouted towards the first car at the motionless man. 'I'm gonna kill you! Kill you good!'

For what seemed an eternity Hickok remained like a statue, standing with both his arms at his sides, defiantly facing his challengers. Only his hair moved as the breeze continued to cut along the railtracks. Then suddenly Hickok started to walk slowly towards Harding.

It was a cold and calculated pace, designed to put the fear of God into his opponents.

'What's eating at you, Byron? You bin hiding for twenty years and suddenly you crawl out from under some rock and come looking for me like some snot-nosed kid. How come?'

'Those were my cowboys you killed!' Harding stepped away from the locomotive with the cocked gun still in his hand. He knew that he could kill the infamous gunfighter before Wild Bill had a chance of drawing either of his weapons, yet there were too many witnesses. Even though his guts were burning with vengeance for his fallen cowboys, he could not shoot even Hickok in cold blood. For he had lived his life by a code of honour that few of his kind respected.

Reluctantly, he holstered the Colt.

'Them boys of yours started it!' Hickok said as the lights from the carriage windows caressed his chiselled features. He walked even closer to the furious man.

'And you finished it, Wild Bill!' Harding spat.

'I always finish it, Byron!' Hickok said. He stopped. There was less than thirty feet in distance between the two adversaries. 'There ain't no prizes in this job for coming second!'

Harding could hear the boots of his men

moving ever closer behind him. He waved his left hand at them and glanced back for the briefest of moments.

'Stay back, boys!' he commanded.

The Triple Bar cowboys obeyed his orders.

As the trail boss returned his attention to the gunfighter he studied the familiar features. They had hardly altered at all. Time had stood still for the infamous Wild Bill Hickok. The hair was still the same. The moustache showed no hint of any grey and the lean body was still as trim as it had been back when he too was a hired gun. A bead of sweat ran down Harding's face.

Yet it was not the appearance of the gunfighter which troubled the trail boss. It was the fact that Hickok still recognized him after so many years that unnerved Harding.

'How come you recall me, Wild Bill?' Harding asked. 'Unlike you, I've aged a tad!'

'I always recall the good guns, Byron,' came the reply. 'You were good. Damn good!'

'I'm gonna kill you, Bill!' Harding repeated his threat. 'I can't let this go!'

There was no emotion in the tall unyielding man who stared straight at the trail boss. No glimmer of anything showed in the original poker-face.

'You got enough boys there with you to try your luck.' Hickok nodded. 'I figured you'd be man enough to face me on your own.'

'I've told them to keep out of this.'

'They won't!' Hickok sighed. 'Just like them other cowboys of yours back in Cheyenne. Not a brain between the whole bunch of them, Byron. I had to kill them 'coz they would have surely killed me if I hadn't.'

Harding flexed the fingers of his right hand when he heard someone clearing his throat above him. His eyes darted to his left and focused on the weathered figure.

'As I live and breathe, if it ain't old Byron Harding!' Tom Dix said as he descended the metal steps to the ground. 'I thought you were dead.'

For the first time in twenty years, Harding felt uneasy.

'Dix?'

'Yep.'

'I heard you'd gone to Boot Hill years back,' Harding said.

'Prison!' Dix corrected as he stood against the body of the railroad car with his thumbs resting on his belt-buckle. 'I went to prison!'

Harding felt uneasy. He was no coward but he was also no fool. He knew that both the men before him were deadly. They had both been fast in their time. As fast as he had been. Were they still as fast? Was he?

Doubt crept over him.

'Give it up, Byron!' Hickok advised. 'There ain't no profit in this.'

Harding knew the tall man was right but he

could not quit now. Not now that he had started. Every ounce of his logical brain told him that the odds were stacked against him but there was something chewing at his craw.

It was either pride or insanity. Or it might have been a blind ambition to prove finally that he was better than the two men into whose shadow he had ridden.

What if he were to outdraw both these living legends?

That would be proof that he was the fastest gun alive. The history books would have to be rewritten. His name would finally be known.

Byron Harding!

He would be the man who killed Wild Bill Hickok and Tom Dix in a deadly showdown. Two against one and he would be victorious.

'I'm calling you both out!' Harding drawled.

Dix straightened up and looked at Hickok.

'I think he's serious, James Butler!'

Hickok nodded.

'Looks that way, Dixie!' Hickok agreed. 'You get back on the train. This is my fight.'

Dix looked at the dozen restless cowboys behind the trail boss. They were already gripping their holstered gun handles ready to join in.

'Looks like the odds are a mite too big for even you this time, James Butler!' Dix said.

'Maybe so!' Wild Bill agreed.

'Let's kill them now, boss!' Vance yelled out

from behind the trail boss.

'Yeah,' Toby agreed. 'They're just two old men! Wild Bill don't look so dangerous to me!'

Harding could hear his men moving towards him.

'I told you all to stay out of this!' he shouted.

'Too much gabbing!' another of the cowboys shouted out.

Then there was a silence that seemed to last an eternity as the cowboys stood to either side of their troubled boss. Tom Dix walked slowly away from the train until he was next to the unblinking Hickok. Neither man uttered another word as they vainly waited for sanity to return to the thirteen men before them.

Then it happened.

All hell broke loose.

TEN

Within seconds of the shooting having started, the engineer and his stoker ducked down in their high cab. The conductor jumped beneath the tender and scrambled across the width of the tracks until he found sanctuary on the other side of the massive locomotive. No thunderstorm could have been more deafening or created as much bloody devastation as did the lethal hail of lead that cut across the distance between Hickok and Dix and the rest of the Triple Bar outfit. Red-hot bullets criss-crossed the distance which separated the well-armed men. Gunsmoke spewed out of every gun barrel as cowboys and gunfighters alike blasted wildly across the thirty or so feet between them.

A showdown could make cowards out of even the bravest of souls. Simply to have the nerve to stand your ground as countless bullets sought your flesh and your very life, was more than most men could or would risk. Yet none of the men who fanned their gun hammers were willing to take even one step backwards or retreat from the battle that had erupted.

Cowboys spun like tops on their heels as they were hit off their feet by the sheer force of the .45s that tore into their dusty bodies.

It was impossible to tell for sure which of the naïve cowboys had drawn and fired first. But whichever of the foolhardy men had squeezed his trigger first, it no longer mattered. The area beside the train was filled with blinding gunsmoke.

Hickok had seen the flash of white lightning and plume of gunsmoke amid the line of cowboys standing shoulder to shoulder with Byron Harding as one of them had fired. As the bullet passed within inches of his lean body, he responded at incredible speed. The two seven-inch-barrelled guns had been cross-drawn from their holsters before a second shot had been fired. With an accuracy that was almost beyond belief, Hickok cut not only Harding down, but the cowboy standing next to him. Again and again he fired as the men before him started to blast their array of weapons.

Tom Dix had felt the heat of the hot lead and threw himself across the ground before dragging his own guns from their holsters.

Bullets tore through the darkness in both directions. The tall gunfighter knelt and continued to fire as shots sliced the air above him. Tom Dix remained on his belly and blasted his weaponry as shots ripped the dusty ground apart to both sides of his prostrate form.

Vance ran at the two experienced gunfighters, firing his Colt with every step. With no sign of emotion on his carved features, Wild Bill raised his left gun and shot the cowboy high in the head. The battered hat flew up as most of Vance's face imploded into a bloody mess.

The body landed in a heap right in front of Hickok. He pushed it on to its side and used it for cover as he continued to fire into the dense black smoke. Terrified cutting-horses dragged their reins free of the branches and galloped into the middle of the shooting. Two leapt over the body Wild Bill was shielding himself with as three more rode straight at Dix. Dix rolled sideways until he felt the wooden sleepers at his back. Dust kicked up off the skittish animals' hoofs as they pounded within inches of the bruised rancher.

Less than two minutes had elapsed since the first shot had been fired. Now it was over. Dust and acrid smoke swirled between the long locomotive and the water-tower as the deadly guns went chillingly silent.

Dix rubbed the grime out of his eyes and tried to focus. The aroma of death was already filling his nostrils. It was a fragrance he knew well.

Hurriedly, Hickok shook the spent shells from both of his red-hot guns and reloaded them. His hooded eyes strained to see through the choking smoke.

'You OK, Dixie?' he called out to his side.

'I think so!' Dix replied. 'What in tarnation happened here, James Butler?'

Hickok snapped both his guns' chambers shut and dragged their hammers back again. He rose slowly to his full height and inhaled deeply.

He did not like the smell which greeted him. It was the smell of death and it had haunted him for more than half his life.

'Somebody started shooting at us, Dixie,' he answered. 'Don't you pay attention?'

Dix holstered one of his Colts and then checked the other. He removed four brass casings and replaced them with bullets from his gunbelt.

'Do you figure it's over?' he asked.

Hickok gritted his teeth.

'I sure hope so! This is getting real tedious!'

Dix got back to his feet as Dan came rushing out of the train carriage and on to the car platform with his gun in his hand. He looked more asleep than awake.

'What's going on, Dixie?' he called out groggily. 'Who's shooting?'

Frantically, Dix waved the barrel of his gun at his partner.

'Get back in there, Dan. Before someone shoots you! Go back to sleep!'

Hickok walked to Dix's side. He still had both his guns aimed towards the pile of cowboys. The gunsmoke was clearing as the gentle breeze swept over the bodies. The sound of groaning filled their ears.

'They ain't all dead, *amigo*!' Dix said.

'I don't give a hoot as long as they quit shooting at us, Dixie!'

Dix nodded.

'Why do you figure they opened up on us, James Butler? I had me the feeling that this was just between you and Harding!'

Hickok started toward them.

'Cowboys! Not a brain between the whole bunch, Dixie!'

The two gunfighters stood above the bodies. Even the darkness could not hide the blood from their knowledgeable eyes. Half were obviously dead. Holes in the head were nearly always fatal. The ones who had taken bullets in the chest fared little better.

'I reckon eight are still alive,' Dix said bluntly as he kicked guns from hands out into the shadows. 'What we gonna do with them?'

'Nothing!' Hickok snapped. 'They'll either die or they'll get up and ride out of here. It's their choice just like it was their choice to start shooting.'

'You OK, Wild Bill!' Dix said.

'I don't get no pleasure out of killing a man like Harding 'coz some cowpoke starts a war for no damn reason!' Hickok replied.

'Harding knew the score.' Dix sighed. 'He

brought these men here. He should have known better.'

'This was between him and me!' Hickok snorted. 'Dumb cowboys!'

'You ain't gonna blame yourself for this slaughter, are you, Bill?'

Hickok did not reply.

He stood like a statue over Byron Harding, glaring down at his handiwork. It did not please him to see a man he had once admired lying with his lead in him. Harding's gun was still in its holster.

Suddenly, the trail boss coughed and opened his eyes. He stared up at the figure hovering over him.

'You ain't any slower than you were back in the old days, Bill!' Harding whispered. 'I should have known that you were too stubborn to slow up.'

'You never even cleared your holster, Byron!' Hickok sighed heavily. 'You used to be so fast it scared even me!'

Harding's eyes seemed to light up.

'Did you ever see me in a shoot-out, Wild Bill? Did you actually see me back in the old days?'

'Yep! Dodge City, about twenty years back. I saw you outdraw one of the Darrow brothers. You were like lightning!' Wild Bill noted. 'The fastest gun I ever saw!'

'The fastest gun?' Harding repeated the words.

'Yep!'

'Faster than even you, Bill?' the trail boss gasped.

Hickok looked at the two neat bullet holes in the man's shirt front. Both were shots that no man could survive.

'Yep, Byron. You were faster than me. That's why I stayed out of your way.'

Harding coughed again. Blood traced down from the corner of his mouth. His head rolled over limply. He was dead.

Tom Dix rested a hand on Hickok's shoulder.

'That was kind of you, Wild Bill.'

Hickok continued to stare at the lifeless man before him.

'What was, Dixie?'

'Telling a dying man that he was faster than you.'

'He was once!' Hickok drawled. 'The trouble is he waited too long to try and prove it!'

ELEVEN

A powerful unseen wind filled the massive black main sail as well as all its lesser cousins. The pirate ship had made good time across the vast expanse of ocean since it had left its latest victim to sink in flames. Only the green bottle-nosed dolphins that frequented the Californian coastal waters could have travelled faster. The *Black Serpent* continued to speed through the afternoon on its course back to Dead Man's Rest with its plundered cargo. The pirates had filled their bellies on their generous rations of confiscated rum and were still eager for the taste of more bloody encounters.

They did not know it but they would not have to wait very long before their insatiable appetite for deadly encounters would again be satisfied.

Unlike his deadly crew Tall Red had better things to do with his time than just drink and revel in the previous day's gruesome thrills.

A plan for something far more profitable than just looting and sinking a naval gunboat for fresh

provisions was already brewing in his fertile imagination. For he had seen fit to strip the *Robert
Armstrong*'s captain of all his maps, charts and offi-
cial papers before placing a bullet between the
naval officer's eyes.

The maps were something Tall Red knew could
prove invaluable to them in the unfamiliar
Californian coastal waters.

For the first time since the pirate ship had
arrived, Tall Red would be able to know exactly
where all the dangerous underwater rocks were
and then ensure that the *Black Serpent* always
steered a course to avoid them.

But it had not been the maps and charts which
had inspired the ruthless sea captain into formu-
lating his most daring plan since they had sailed
unnoticed into these waters. They were just icing
on the cake.

Tall Red sat with his back to the large open
window in his luxurious cabin amid the trophies
that he and his predecessors had taken by force.
Less ambitious men would have retired by now and
simply lived off the wealth which surrounded
them. But not Tall Red. He was driven by something more vicious than just plain ordinary greed.

Since he had first ridden the Wild West as an
outlaw he had known that there was never enough
money to satisfy his kind. He had been forced to
stow away on a cargo ship when the law had trailed
him night and day for nearly a month until there

was no more land left to ride upon. The sea had saved his life and he owed it a debt he knew he could never repay.

What he had become was something far more honest than most of his contemporaries who had remained to face one posse after another. He did not even try and hide the fact that it was not the prize which was important to him and his fellow-pirates. It was the thrill of the chase. The sheer power he felt in his guts when everything fell together like the pieces of a complicated jigsaw puzzle. Even being hunted at sea was exciting, unlike being chased on land. For to captain a vessel like the *Black Serpent* and outmanoeuvre another ship on the high seas was in itself a feat not easily bettered. To be able to turn the tables on your hunter was even better.

He lived to kill; to wallow in the glory of his own depraved lust for everything most men would consider horrific.

Above all, Tall Red knew his thirst for blood could never be quenched.

For hours the *Black Serpent*'s captain had mulled over one salvaged chart after another with the small group of his most trusted men.

Men who shared his own depraved relish for the adventure their life provided. Men who had proved their loyalty and courage in battle.

The tattooed Skin was there as always. Like a faithful hound, he never strayed far from his captain's side. A man who protected the back of the man with the flowing red beard and mane. No man had ever managed to get the drop on Tall Red since Skin had been with him. Those who had been foolish enough to try had been dealt with swiftly by the murderous pirate, a man who, like Tall Red, had once been wanted dead or alive throughout the West.

John Morgan and Curly Wilde, the two master helmsmen, made notes silently over Tall Red's shoulder before moving to the captain's table and studying the detailed naval charts and maps. Their job was to calculate as many safe courses to and from their hidden harbour as were possible with such a long vessel as the *Black Serpent*.

They held the lives of every one of the pirates in their skilled hands. Both had spent their entire lives at sea on both sides of the law. Whatever reasons had drawn them to sail under the black flag, only they knew. Like most of their fellow-pirates it would remain a secret that they would protect to the bitter end.

Only one of the assembled pirates seemed to have his mind elsewhere. The muscular dark-skinned creature with a face and body covered in scars brooded in a corner of the cabin. He sat on the floor and listened to every word the others uttered.

But he never joined in any of the discussions, for he did not care to think. That was not his strong point. He just did as the others commanded.

He killed.

His strong fingers toyed with a jewel-encrusted Toledo steel dagger and ran its honed blade over his arms and head continuously. It was as if he did not want any body-hair to hide his cruel scars. They were like badges of courage to the huge pirate.

Proof of what he had once been and still was.

Evidence of his bloodthirsty existence.

There was no other as deadly as Khan aboard the *Black Serpent*. Yet no one ever discovered where Khan had originally come from. There were no hints of an accent in his deep voice. Or perhaps Khan had absorbed a small part of all his fellow-pirates' accents until his own had virtually disappeared.

Some recalled hearing him speak in a strange tongue that none could recognize.

He had joined the *Black Serpent* in Java with six other equally well-built creatures. All appeared to have been cast from the same mysterious mould. They had all been experts in killing and seemed capable of fighting with any weapon that came to hand.

It was the jewelled daggers that had always seen the most action, created the most gore. Since men had first learned how to forge metal, the daggers had become the preferred weapon of the silent destroyers.

But that had been a few years earlier. Countless

deadly battles ago. Now, of his small group, only Khan remained. Since the last of his own kind had been slain, Khan had hardly spoken at all.

The small brown eyes set in the large face chilled the rest of the men inside the captain's cabin, but none objected to Khan being there. He was the one pirate who fought without any consideration for his own safety. Injury or even death held no fear for the large man.

Khan was a mystery. One that even Tall Red was not brave enough to try and figure out.

Tall Red lifted the small leather satchel he had taken from the *Robert Armstrong* captain's cabin off the floor and used a small knife to prize its lock open.

'What you got there, Tall Red?' Skin asked.

The pirate captain's eyebrows tightened as he studied the collection of private letters and documents. Then the hint of a smile traced across his face.

'This is interesting, boys,' Tall Red said. 'Damn interesting.'

Skin moved to the captain's side as he read.

'It's just a bunch of words. I thought you had some picture-book, Tall Red.'

Tall Red sat forward and discarded most of the papers until his hands held on tightly to just one. He glanced at Morgan and Wilde. A twisted smile could be seen hiding somewhere beneath the scarlet beard.

'Find out where San Remo is on one of those maps, boys.' Curly Wilde searched the charts as Morgan moved closer to their smiling captain.

'What you found there, Tall Red?' he asked, trying to read over the pirate captain's shoulder. 'You found something juicy, I'll wager!'

Tall Red smiled broadly. His teeth flashed almost as brightly as his eyes.

'If I ain't mistaken I just found us the golden goose, I'll bet,' Tall Red replied. He stood and waved the sheet of paper in his hand under their noses. 'This is one real valuable scrap of paper.'

'Is it a treasure map?' Skin asked innocently.

'As good as any treasure map Black Beard ever scrawled.' Tall Red grinned. 'This is the key to open up a golden padlock.'

There was a look of confusion on Skin's face.

'What you talkin' about?'

'I found it!' Wilde said, his tobacco-stained index finger pressing down on one of the charts. 'San Remo! There it is, but I don't know why ya want to find it for. Just a small port above the border to Mexico.'

The men gathered around the helmsman and stared at the seemingly insignificant name on the map of the Californian coastline.

'What do you want to know about that little place for?' John Morgan asked. 'It looks too small for the *Black Serpent* to dock at.'

'And where are we now?' Tall Red enquired

101

gazing down at the map. 'What's our present position?'

John Morgan leaned over and placed his own finger down on the chart.

'Roughly, we're about there.'

'Yep. That's about it.' Curly Wilde nodded.

Tall Red was excited.

'Where's San Francisco? Find it.'

Again Wilde found the name first. He slid his finger to the neatly printed name.

'There! You ain't thinking of taking the *Black Serpent* in there, are you? It's a natural harbour full of ships and a lot of them are US Navy gunboats!'

'Where do you figure Dead Man's Rest is?' the captain continued.

John Morgan pointed to an unmarked part of the coast on the chart somewhere between the two ports.

'It has to be somewhere around there. Why?'

Tall Red laughed and marched around the table littered in rolls of charts. He waved the sheet of paper above his head and winked at all four of the men in turn. They were all confused with the exception of Khan. Khan simply did not care.

'What you so happy about, Tall Red?' Morgan asked nervously. 'What you got planned?'

'Do you know the date, boys?'

'There ain't no way we can tell the date, Captain.' Wilde shrugged. 'It don't matter none to us, does it?'

'Every day is the same out here, Tall Red!' Skin said.

'It's the third of the month,' Tall Red told them. 'The third.'

'How can you possibly know that?' John Morgan smiled broadly. 'And what does it matter?'

'How do I know it's the third? 'Coz I stole the captain's log off that navy boat' Tall Red answered. 'I was reading it earlier and noted the last entry the captain made. Last night. That was the second. So today is the third. Right?'

'Right.' Skin sat down.

'So what?' Khan muttered as he slid his razor-sharp dagger over his chin. 'Numbers no good.'

Tall Red looked down at the seated pirate.

'Because the letter in my hand tells me that every month on the fifth of every month, the army sends a chest full of gold coin from Pier thirty-three in San Francisco to San Remo by an ordinary paddle-steamer. The trip takes her exactly four days to reach San Remo according to this letter!'

'So that means she reaches San Remo on the ninth!' Morgan shrugged as he studied the charts before him. 'We got more than enough time to set a course for San Remo and lie in wait for the Santa Catalina, Tall Red.'

Skin rushed to the smiling captain.

'How much gold coin, Tall Red?'

'Enough to pay a couple of thousand soldier boys a month's wages, Skin.' Tall Red smiled.

'That has to be an awful lot of money, Captain.'
Tall Red grinned.

'Damn right, Skin. That's one hell of a lot of money just begging to be stolen.'

'We going to steal it?' Skin asked.

'Is there killing for me, Captain?' Khan asked.

Tall Red nodded to both questions, then moved to his helmsmen and draped his arms over their shoulders. 'How long do you reckon it would take us to reach San Remo, boys?'

'With our sails full of wind like they are?' Morgan grinned.

'About a day and a half at most!' Wilde chuckled.

'I reckon we should anchor off San Remo and wait for that little old paddle-steamer to bring that gold to us.' Tall Red nodded. 'What you boys reckon?'

'Aye, Captain. Perfect,' John Morgan answered. 'With the charts and maps me and Curly can plot an exact course and even work out the paddle-steamer's exact route. We will just have to sit and wait.'

'The fly will come to our web, boys!' Tall Red chuckled. He grabbed a bottle of rum off the table and swigged heartily.

'A pretty fat fly, Captain!' Skin rubbed his hands together eagerly.

'Set a course, boys!' Tall Red commanded.

'Aye, Captain!' Morgan grabbed hold of one of

the charts, led Wilde out of the cabin and up towards the deck.

Tall Red pushed the letter into his shirt aad then raised the bottle to his lips again.

'Damn! I sure enjoy being a pirate!' He grinned.

TWELVE

The *Santa Catalina* paddle-steamer had seen better days, like its captain and crew. It was small by Mississippi standards and that was its attraction to the authorities. The army had used the same vessel for nearly a decade because of its unassuming appearance.

They did not want to advertise the king's ransom they were sending from the United States branch mint by sea to San Remo every month. So far no one had suspected anything. To transport so much freshly minted gold coin for the army garrisons' salaries in anything that might attract attention of the thousands of less than honest souls who frequented the notorious San Francisco quaysides might be considered foolhardy.

Few gave the *Santa Catalina* a second look. It was not the most fashionable of vessels to ply the coastal waters. Only those who wanted to go to San Remo would purchase a ticket for the three-to-four-day journey. Those with bulging wallets and self-conceit to match would take the more stylish and expensive vessels that were tied up in the bay along the many piers.

During the previous decade the unassuming vessel had been used to transport the valuable wooden chest from San Franciso to the small port of San Remo once every month. No one had even imagined the riches that the weathered paddle-steamer was carrying. The army had ensured that any overly inquisitive crooked eyes that might accidentally stray to the covered wagon with its small cavalry escort going to the *Santa Catalina*, would also see three identical wagons and mounted soldiers taking a large box aboard various other ships along the line of piers.

So far, nobody had guessed which were the decoys and which was the real money-chest. It seemed obvious that so much money would be put on the fastest ships. Ships which were invulnerable to the shore rats that littered the streets. The pitifully aged paddle-steamer was never seriously considered as being anything except a pathetic decoy.

The huge locomotive had circled the wide natural bay and arrived on schedule opposite the pier entrances early on the morning of the fifth. Scores of well-paid cowpokes went about their duties and forced the dazed and confused steers out of the freight cars.

A dozen cattle-agents were there to ensure their

clients' beef on the hoof was guided in the right directions. The acrid aroma of the cattle-cars was choking. In all it took more than three hours to unload all the steers from the stinking cars.

But Hickok, Dix and Shaw had not waited in line like the well-tailored cattle-agents. After purchasing tickets for San Remo aboard the *Santa Catalina*, the tall gunfighter had paid the train conductor a twenty-dollar Double Eagle gold piece to make sure that the massive bull and their three horses were taken to Pier 33 to the steamer and secured on its aft deck behind the huge paddle-wheel.

Wild Bill had never been to this famous city before, but he could smell hard liquor a mile off and led his two companions straight to the nearest bar, which was built into the façades of the closest piers, opposite the line of stock-cars.

'This looks like an interesting little saloon, boys!' Hickok had said as he pushed open the solid door and entered the busy barroom. Neither Tom Dix or Dan Shaw had argued the point. The room was similar to the saloons they were used to, but there was a subtle difference. For this place was filled with men who worked on the hundreds of ships berthed along the piers and out in the congested bay.

Men who played almost as hard as they worked.

For hours Hickok had quietly drunk his whiskey beside Dix and Dan and watched the train through a large decorated window. He had somehow managed to ignore the snide comments aimed in his direction until they no longer came. But the gunfighter's interest was not on anything outside the smoke-filled building. Slowly Wild Bill's attention was drawn to the other men inside the large bar.

There seemed to be poker-games in progress on at least half the tables. Temptingly large piles of chips were stacked high in all directions. Well-built stevedores played poker and downed countless glasses of frothy beer less than twenty feet from the window. Hickok ran a finger along the length of his moustache and stood up.

'What you doing, James Butler?' Dix asked. 'Our boat sails in an hour or so!'

'Don't fret, Dixie.' Hickok smiled. He placed a cigar between his teeth and struck a match along the edge of their table. He sucked in its flame and then exhaled a long line of grey smoke before tossing the match away. 'Reckon I'll go and relieve them gents of their salaries!'

'Don't go getting into no trouble, Bill,' Dan begged. Wild Bill winked.

'Trust me. I'm a professional!'

'A professional trouble-finder!' Dix sighed.

Dix and Shaw remained at their table as their companion walked across the sawdust-covered floor to the closest of the card-players. He stood and rested his hands on the back of an empty hardback chair.

'Who or what are you, mister?' asked a stevedore called Flynn as he stared up at the flamboyant Hickok. 'A cowboy or something?'

Hickok gripped the cigar firmly in his mouth.

'I'm no cowboy!'

'I know who you are!' one of the others said, pointing with the stem of his pipe. 'You're that dude. I seen ya picture on dime novels, ain't I.'

Hickok nodded.

'That you have, *amigo*! I've had me a lot of books written about my adventures over the years!'

'That's right!' Flynn chipped in. 'You're Buffalo Bill!'

Hickok bit hard on his cigar and glanced at Dix and Dan. They were smiling far wider than he liked.

'Yep, I'm Buffalo Bill. I should have known I'd not be able to pull the wool over your eyes.'

'We ain't dumb, ya know!' Flynn nodded hard.

'Can anyone sit in?' Hickok asked politely.

The four heavily constructed card-players all pulled their cards to their chests and looked at the tall gunfighter.

'Don't ya know anything about poker, Bill?' asked a man called Kelly. 'You can't sit in when a hand is being played.'

Hickok raised an eyebrow.

'I can't? Why not?'

'Rules!' another of the men, called Williams, added.

Wild Bill sighed and went to turn away.

'I'm sorry. I've never actually played poker before. I didn't know. I apologize.'

'Hold ya horses, Bill,' Kelly said with a wink to his pals. 'I reckon you can sit down. It ain't your fault ya don't know the rules.'

'Why, thank you kindly, gents.' Hickok pulled the chair away from the table and sat down. He removed his cigar from his mouth and tapped the ash off its glowing tip. He then returned it to his mouth and puffed.

'You can join in the next game. OK?' Williams smiled.

Hickok pulled out his billfold and opened it.

'Is a hundred dollars enough to play?' he asked coyly.

The four men all grinned and passed glances at one another.

'Certainly!' Williams chuckled.

Hickok nodded.

'Good! I sure hope you boys will teach me this interesting game. It looks a lot of fun.'

'We'll teach you, Buffalo,' another of the card players called Smith gruffed. 'We'll teach you good.'

Hickok turned his head and looked at Dix and Dan. They both seemed to shake their heads at the same time. He smiled and returned his attention to the card players.

'That's fine. Mighty fine.'

111

*

The sound of the *Santa Catalina*'s whistle could be plainly heard inside the barroom. Yet only Dix and Dan seemed to hear its spirited call. The ranchers rose and made their way through the crowd of men gathered around the card-table where Hickok was still seated.

They looked down at the table. It seemed that every gaming-chip was in the centre of the table. Only Flynn and Hickok were still holding their cards as they eyed each other.

'There must be four hundred bucks in the pot, Bill!' Flynn muttered as he scratched the side of his face and shuffled his five cards continuously. 'I ain't got no more money. I sure hope you ain't the sort to try and steal the pot.'

Hickok looked straight at his last remaining opponent.

'I don't steal, *amigo*. Show your hand and I'll show mine.'

Both men placed their cards face up on the table.

Flynn had three aces but Wild Bill had four tens.

'You won!' the stevedore gasped.

Hickok sat upright.

'I did?'

'You did!' Williams nodded from his chair.

'Cash my chips in, boys!' Hickok smiled as he rose to his full impressive height.

112

Smith added up the chips and then counted out the $400 in grubby bills.

'There ya go.'

Wild Bill scooped up his winnings and placed them inside his billfold. He then saw Dix and Dan.

'What's wrong, Dixie?'

'The boat's blowing its whistle, Bill,' Dix said. 'We gotta go. She's about to sail.'

Hickok turned to the card-players and touched the brim of his hat to each of them.

'It's bin an education, boys. I thank you kindly.'

The four men nodded. They were neither happy or angry. They seemed dazed.

'See ya, Buffalo!' Flynn said.

Hickok, Dix and Dan walked out of the bar and quickly headed for Pier 33.

'Look on the bright side, Flynn,' Smith said with a shrug. 'At least we can say we was fleeced by Buffalo Bill.'

'Reckon so,' Flynn agreed.

Williams rubbed his neck and bit his lip.

'He sure learned poker quick!'

'That's 'coz he's Buffalo Bill,' Kelly added.

The three other card-players all nodded silently.

THIRTEEN

There was only one thing on Tom Dix's mind as he ascended the wide stern gangway quickly. Dix led his two friends straight to their animals. The three horses seemed skittish as they eyed the huge well-secured bull across the desk. Hickok and Dan watched Dix move to the side of the large beast and tighten the rope attached to its nose-ring.

'Keep it good and tight, Dixie,' Wild Bill said. 'We don't him getting loose, do we.'

Dix looped another knot in the rope that was strung through the metal girder-eyes and tightened it. He then checked the leather shackles and chains that held the beast's legs together.

'Damn right, James Butler. I figure this boy could tear the whole boat apart if he got upset. Best not to take chances.'

Dan Shaw checked the horses.

'How rough do ya figure it gets out there on the sea, boys?'

Dix smiled.

'Real rough!'

'That sure is one hell of a big bull you got there, Dixie,' Hickok noted as he rested his back against the taffrail and studied the quayside. 'Reckon my pal Kirby Jones has got himself a bargain there. Eight hundred dollars ain't much money for such a big old critter.'

'As long as we do get eight hundred dollars!' Dix sighed. 'We lost every damn penny of our money to them bankers. That big hunk of prime steak is all we got left to our name.'

'We sure appreciate you paying for the train and boat tickets, Bill.' Dan said.

'Heck,' Hickok boomed out at the top of his lungs. 'I just covered all my expenses in that card-game. In fact I reckon I'm in profit.'

'We still owe you, James Butler,' Dix said as he tied their trio of saddles together near the horses.

Hickok suddenly spotted a covered wagon with a cavalry escort coming along the quay. He went silent and stared at the troopers as they dismounted and went to the back of the wagon.

'Army boys!' Dan frowned. 'I sure hate army boys.'

'I shot me a few of the varmints a couple years back.' Wild Bill chuckled. 'The jury found me not guilty, though.'

Dix leaned against the railings and stared hard at the men.

'They sure are a busy bunch.'

'What do think they're up to, boys?' Hickok asked under his breath.

Dan studied the men as they hauled a heavy wooden box out of the wagon and started up the gangplank.

'Mighty interesting, Wild Bill,' Dan said.

'What do you figure them soldier boys got there?' Hickok wondered aloud. 'Whatever it is it must be mighty valuable to warrant an armed escort!'

'Must be money,' Dix said.

'Gold,' Hickok added. 'Them boys' legs are buckling under the weight of that box. Only gold is that heavy.'

'Gold and lead.' Dan smiled.

Hickok chuckled.

'Since when does the US Army escort a box full of lead, Daniel?'

The retired lawman shrugged.

'You gotta point there.'

The four troopers waved their pistols at the three onlookers as they headed to the first cabin and entered. A few moments later only two of the soldiers came out and the sound of the door being bolted echoed along the deck.

Hickok went towards the pair of nervous soldiers as they stepped up on to the wide gangway. Again, pistols were aimed in his direction. The gunfighter's hooded eyes narrowed.

'Best not aim them hoglegs at me, boys!' he warned. 'I've killed men for less.'

'You ain't seen nothin' here, mister!' the soldier closest to the gunfighter snarled as they both stopped. 'OK? This never happened! Understand?'

Hickok stared hard at the soldier.

'I reckon you got a big mouth there, son!'

Both soldiers stared at the grim-faced Hickok.

'Who are you, mister?' the first trooper asked.

Wild Bill stepped closer to the angry soldier and swiftly grabbed the gun from his hand. He emptied the bullets from it and then rammed the weapon into the man's chest. The trooper gasped as his eyes watered.

'I'm the man who just disarmed you, sonny!'

'What's ya name?' The soldier coughed. 'I'm making out a report on you!'

'This is the famous Buffalo Bill Cody,' Tom Dix interrupted. 'He don't mean no harm.'

'Buffalo Bill?' The other trooper repeated the name. 'Gosh, Clancy. This guy's a legend. He killed a lot of Indians!'

'And buffaloes!' Dix added.

Hickok smiled as both men continued on back to the shore. His expression drastically altered when he overheard the first trooper's next comment.

'Looks like one of them powdered actors to me!'

The army wagon was turned and headed back up to the street with its mounted escort to either side of it.

117

'Easy, Bill!' Dan said. 'They were just kids.'

Wild Bill Hickok turned and stared at the locked cabin door with the number 1 painted on its dark surface.

'They're old enough for killing, Dan!' Hickok commented. He strode off along the outer deck in the direction of the bow.

'Where's he headed, Dixie?'

Dix glanced at his partner.

'Must be a well-stocked bar up there someplace. He's just following his nose.'

They both trailed him along the boarded deck as two Mexican sailors started to pull on ropes and haul the gangplank up. They secured it to the cast-iron uprights as two well-built dock workers cast their lines free. Before the ranchers had reached the bow, the huge paddle-wheel had started to rotate and the steamer moved slowly away from the quayside.

'Looks like we're on our way to San Remo, Dan,' Dix commented as the converted river-boat made its way out into the harbour on a course which would take it around the large uninhabited island of Alcatraz before heading out of the bay and into the Pacific.

Dan paused and stared ahead. A dense fog hung like a blanket over the water beyond the mouth of the famous bay.

'That don't look too inviting, Dixie,' he said, rubbing his chin. 'In fact it looks like trouble to me.'

'So does that!' Dix tapped his pal's arm and stared into the large room which was both dining-area and barroom.

Dan Shaw frowned, then looked to where his friend was indicating with small nods of his head. He could see the unmistakable figure of Wild Bill propped up against the bar counter.

'I see him. So what?' Dan queried.

'Not Hickok.' Dix sighed before turning his partner's head slightly until he could see a man dressed almost as boldly as Wild Bill. 'Him!'

'Who's that?'

'That's Bonanza Bob Sherman,' Dix replied.

'You know him?'

'Yep!' Dix gritted his teeth.

'What is he?'

'He's a gambler by trade but he's also a thief and a crack shot.' Tom Dix pulled the safety loops off his gun hammers before entering the room with Dan next to his left shoulder. 'He's also big trouble.'

Bonanza Bob turned and stared hard at the weathered figure.

'I don't hardly believe my eyes. Is that you, Tom Dix?' he called across the room.

'Yep. It's me, Bob,' Dix answered as he stopped and turned to face the man who, he knew, was as deadly with his guns as he himself was. 'Long time since our trails crossed.'

'I heard you were dead, Dix!' Bonanza Bob

smiled.

'It's only a matter of time.' Tom Dix nodded.

Hickok turned and observed the man in a well-tailored frock-coat approaching his two friends. He squinted hard, then recognized the face he had not seen for nearly twenty years.

'Bonanza Bob Sherman!' he roared at the top of his voice. 'You low-life gutter-rat!'

Sherman's smile evaporated. His eyes darted to Hickok.

'Wild Bill?'

Hickok strode abruptly away from the bar and stopped next to Dix and Dan. He raised a hand and pointed a finger straight at Sherman's face.

'You tried to have me killed, Bonanza!' he shouted. 'Damn near succeeded as well.'

'That was just a joke, Wild Bill.' Sherman forced a smile.

'I didn't laugh!' Hickok snorted like a bull ready to charge. 'I got wounded!'

'What he do?' Dix asked.

'He set a posse on me!' Hickok fumed. 'He convinced the law up in Black Rock that I was a desperado, wanted dead or alive. He got them to pay him for the information!'

Bonanza Bob shrugged.

'I needed a few bucks to get into a big poker-game, Bill. You'd have done the same.'

Dix and Dan held on to Hickok as he raged forward towards the unrepentant Sherman.

'Easy, James Butler. Easy,' Dix whispered in his ear. 'We can't afford no more trouble. Not until after we get to San Remo and sells that bull.'

Hickok stopped.

'You're right. It was a long time ago after all. Reckon I'll turn the other cheek.'

'You got religion, Wild Bill?' Bonanza Bob mocked. 'Well, I declare.'

'Yep! I got me religion OK, Bonanza,' Hickok whispered. His eyes burned across the distance between Sherman and himself.

'You going to behave yourself if we let go of you?' Dix asked.

'Sure enough!'

The ranchers released their hold on the tall gunfighter. He turned away from Sherman and then dropped his right shoulder. Then suddenly Wild Bill swung on his high-heeled boots and threw a clenched right fist with all his strength at the still smiling Sherman.

The punch caught the jaw perfectly.

There was a cracking noise as teeth snapped off under the powerful impact.

'You stopped smiling, Bonanza!' Hickok said before he repeated the punch with his left fist.

Bonanza Bob Sherman went staggering backwards until he hit a table. He toppled over it and landed in a heap.

'An eye for an eye!' Hickok laughed.

'He ain't gonna like that, Bill,' Dan said. 'He

might try and get even.'

'He's gotta wake up first!' Hickok nodded and kissed his red knuckles.

'That ought to take a while!' Dix shrugged.

The paddle-steamer lurched and all three men watched as glasses slid off a table as if driven by some unseen hand.

'I sure hope I don't regret coming on this boat with you boys!' Hickok said. He headed back to the bar.

'There's nothing to worry about,' Dix said, resting his elbows on the bar counter.

A young Mexican sailor entered the large room and looked at the barman.

'The captain say to batten down the hatches, Pedro!' he said in a shaking voice. 'He say we are headed into a big storm maybe!'

Hickok lifted a whiskey bottle off the bar and filled three glasses.

'What was that you were saying, Dixie?'

FOURTEEN

It was three days since the paddle-steamer had left the foggy waters of San Francisco harbour and ventured out into the deep, unpredictable waters of the Pacific Ocean. At barely over twelve knots the aged steamer was far slower than most vessels which hugged the ragged coastline on their regular journeys to and from the notorious seaport. An eerie fog had hung over the waters since the slow-moving boat had started its voyage. It was getting worse as the sea grew more hostile.

Dix and Dan watered and fed the three horses and then the large bull. The boat began to rock beneath their feet. It was becoming harder to walk on the flat deck as waves swept up over the low-sided steamer.

Dix stared at the sea.

'Looks like a storm is brewing up.'

Unable to maintain his balance, Shaw sat down on one of the large wooden cargo-boxes that were secured near the boat's bulkhead.

'Sit down and rest your bones, Dixie.'

Tom Dix smiled and did as he was told.

'Where's Wild Bill?'

'Last time I saw him he was sitting at a card-table drinking his fill of whiskey.'

'What about Bonanza Bob?'

Dix glanced at the waves which were rolling higher than the height of the small paddle-boat.

'Do you reckon them two boys will lock horns again?'

Dan raised an eyebrow. 'I sure hope not!'

'You and me both!'

'Something else is troubling you, Dixie!' Dan continued. 'What you brooding about?'

'A question's been nagging at my craw, Dan,' Dix said. 'Why is Bonanza Bob on this boat?'

Dan looked at his partner.

'Maybe he wants to go to San Remo,' Dan suggested. 'That town is only a few miles from the army garrison. A poker-player like him could make a lot of money from fleecing troopers of their wages.'

Dix nodded. The boat jolted beneath the boxes upon which they were sitting. He sat upright and leaned against the wooden bulkhead behind him.

'You could be right but I have this sneaking feeling that he might have his eye on an easier pot.'

'Are you talking about the army strongbox?' Shaw asked. 'I can't see Bob trying anything out here at sea. He'd have to get it back to shore.'

Dix nodded at these words.

'He could take the lifeboat or even use this old crate to go to a safe port, Dan.'

'Are you serious?' asked Shaw.

'Dead serious.'

'Even so, it ain't none of our business,' Dan exhaled. 'The soldiers in that cabin are well-armed. They'd blast him to hell if he tried anything, old friend.'

'If Bob does try his luck, he'll have to start killing,' Dix explained. 'It won't end with them two soldiers. He'll have to kill the witnesses and then the captain and his crew.'

'I see what you mean.'

'He's on this boat for some reason.' Dix frowned. 'I know Bonanza Bob Sherman. I've seen him work. He ain't like most hired gunslingers. He's greedy, Dan. And sometimes he's a tad too ambitious for his own good.'

'I thought that he was just a gambler and a hired gun, Dixie.' Shaw gripped the pipe stem in his teeth. 'He's not a cold-blooded killer, is he?'

'Don't let them fancy clothes fool you. He'd kill you and steal your teeth if there was gold in them.'

Dan rubbed his whiskered jaw.

'Would he try anything with you and Wild Bill aboard?'

Dix shrugged.

'Like I said, sometimes he can get a tad ambitious.'

Again the entire paddle-steamer jolted as if hit by something far stronger than just ordinary waves. Dix rose, staggered to the rails and stared down hard into the water which lashed up and over the *Santa Catalina.*

'I'm sure that I just seen something damn big down there in the water, Dan!'

'Like what?'

'I don't know. Something big!'

'You're tired, Dixie! Your eyes can play tricks on you,' Dan said. He joined his friend and looked at the water and the waves, which were getting more and more restless around them. 'I don't see nothing.'

Dix raised his left hand until it shaded his eyes from the low sun.

'The sky don't look too good either. It'll be dark soon and them waves are getting bigger all the time,' he observed. 'I figure we're already headed straight down the throat of a storm.'

'You're right.' Dan Shaw looked forward. His pal was correct. There were black storm-clouds swirling in the sky a mile or so ahead of the paddle-steamer. Forks of lightning splintered down out of the clouds. 'Reckon we're surrounded.'

'I sure wish it was Apaches.' Dix forced a half-hearted smile. 'I'd know what to do then. But what do you do when it's the weather that's got a lasso on you?'

'Let's get back to Wild Bill,' Dan suggested.

'Have us a couple of games of five-card stud.'

Dix nodded. He was about to follow when he caught a glimpse of something out in the waves. He grabbed Dan's shoulder and pointed.

'What was that, Dan?'

'What?' Shaw asked. 'What you pointing at?'

'Didn't you see it?' Dix staggered across the rocking deck until he reached the railings. He gripped them firmly and squinted hard. 'I saw something out there in them waves.'

'What did you see, Dixie?'

'I ain't sure. All I know is that it was black and it was big.'

Dan held on to the rails beside his pal. He screwed up his eyes and looked out at the rolling waves. The sun was low and the dark cloudy sky cast a million shadows over the restless waters.

'I don't see a thing.'

Dix shook his head. Rain started to drift over the *Santa Catalina*. It burned their eyes and made it even harder to focus on the waves.

'It broke surface and then disappeared again.'

'It could have been a whale,' Shaw suggested. 'I read someplace that the ocean is full of the critters. Some of them are as big as saloons.'

'You read too much, Dan!'

Both men were about to move away from the side of the paddle-boat when one of the Mexican sailors called Ramon walked up to them. He looked at the veteran gunfighter knowingly.

'That was no whale, Señor Dixie,' he said in a low whisper that chilled both men.

'Then what was it, Ramon?' Dix asked.

The crewman's eyes widened. He stood on tiptoe and stretched up until the top of his head almost reached Dix's unshaven chin.

'Monsters, Señor Dixie!' he whispered. 'Sea monsters!'

FIFTEEN

There had been no time for Dix and Dan to play even a single hand of poker as they sat down with the stern-faced Hickok. A massive wave crashed into the starboard side of the *Santa Catalina* and shook the entire boat. Water washed through the large room. It knocked tables and chairs aside before washing out of the door opposite. The sound of wooden panels cracking into a million splinters echoed throughout the vessel. Dix leapt back to his feet.

'Easy, Dixie!' Wild Bill muttered. His hooded eyes darted to the shocked rancher. 'It's only a storm!'

'Don't you ever get excited, James Butler?' Dix asked. A fraction of a second later the boat lurched and the half-consumed bottle of whiskey slid off the card-table into Hickok's left hand.

'Not often, Dixie.' The gunfighter smiled.

The sound of their distressed animals filled their ears as the paddle-steamer laboured in the rough seas. Dan forced himself upright and followed Dix out on to the soaked decks.

Hickok turned, took a swig from the bottle and glared at Bonanza Bob near the bar counter. Both men were getting liquored-up in preparation for something.

'Weather seems to be getting a tad frisky, Bob,' Hickok said in a low drawl.

Bonanza Bob touched his bruised jaw and then raised his own whiskey-bottle to his bloodstained lips. He did not reply. He simply drank and continued to watch the man who had not only knocked him out, but had also managed to snap four of his teeth off at the gum-line.

The sky was filled with violent black clouds. They loomed over the normally calm waters like an ancient prophecy of impending doom. Shafts of deadly lightning could be seen off in the distance, yet there was no sound of thunder to be heard. The paddle-steamer was being buffeted by strangely unseasonal and strong waves. It was like a mere toy in a child's bathwater. Both ranchers knew, as they made their way to the stern, that the captain up in the wheelhouse had to be fighting just to maintain control of the damaged vessel.

Dix and Dan reached the paddle-steamer's aft deck just in time to be knocked off their feet by another large wave which came out of the darkness that surrounded them. Dix felt himself hit the railings and grabbed them with his gloved hands as

Dan Shaw crashed into him. Both men were soaked to the skin as they floated helplessly on their backs. Then the water drained off the boat.

Dix dragged himself up and tried to cough out the salty water that he had unwillingly swallowed.

'You OK, Dan?'

Dan Shaw used the railing to pull his sodden body off the deck. He gasped heavily.

'We should make sure the animals are well lashed down,' Dix said as the sky above them erupted into a deafening roar.

As if from nowhere, the drenched Ramon appeared on hands and knees beside the two exhausted ranchers. Dix assisted the youngster to his bare feet.

'You OK, son?' Dix asked.

'This is very bad, *señor*!' Ramon said in a stammering voice. 'This weather is not normal, *amigos*!'

'We already figured that, Ramon!' Dan patted the terrified youth's wet back.

The merciless storm was showing no sign of relenting. One moment the *Santa Catalina* was tossed upward and the next it fell into an abyss.

The paddle-steamer rolled helplessly as the mountainous waves grew more and more angry.

Dix groped his way along the railings until he found the three saddles tethered together. He reached down and unhooked a rope from one saddle horn.

'What you doing, Dixie?' Dan called out. He was

clinging to the side of the boat as it continued to twist and turn on the waves.

Dix looped his left arm around the metal upright and steadied himself. His skilled hands started to uncoil the rope until he had a lasso large enough to fit over his broad shoulders. He slipped it around his waist and tightened it. Then he tied the other end of his rope to the metal upright.

'Now if I get tossed off this crate into that sea, haul me back! OK?' Dix shouted above the unearthly sound of the storm which had engulfed them.

Dan and Ramon nodded and gripped the railings tightly. They watched as Dix forced his way through the mixture of sea spray and driving rain across the slippery deck towards their frightened livestock.

'What's he doing, Señor Dan?' Ramon asked the watchful rancher beside him.

'Risking his scrawny neck again, son!' Dan Shaw answered.

'But why?'

' 'Coz them animals are all we got in the world, Ramon.' Dan staggered to the saddles and removed the other pair of saddle ropes. He handed one to the wide-eyed sailor.

'Use this to tie yourself to the railings, Ramon!'

'Señor Dix is very brave, *amigo*!'

Dan uncoiled the rope in his hands.

'He's got vinegar, son!'

132

*

The *Santa Catalina* was not built for this type of punishment. It was being thrown from one wave to another as its paddle-wheel repeatedly found itself out of the turbulent water. The storm had grown worse. Far worse than any of the steamer's crew had ever experienced before. The rain continued to drive down like unseen needles. The two cattle ranchers had spent most of the night trying to protect their animals from the ever worsening storm.

Like the bull and the horses, they were bruised and bloodied.

Most of the lights in the lanterns had long been extinguished by the waves that appeared to hit the helpless boat from every conceivable direction at once. The few lanterns which stubbornly managed to keep their wicks dry swung so vigorously that their light only added to the confusion.

Hour after hour the three men had battled unseen powers to prevent the large bull from being injured. They had fought with the chains to ensure that the beast could not move more than a few inches from where they had shackled it.

Their three long-legged mounts were not so easily protected, though. The terrified horses wanted nothing more than to escape from the exposed aft end of the storm-battered vessel. Yet the more they fought against their bonds, the more their hoofs slid on the slippery wooden deck. Wave after crushing wave crashed down on to the paddle-boat.

There was a merciless fury at work.

The power of the water was so focused, it smashed the cargo boxes into a million splinters. No mythical giant could have inflicted more destruction. The foaming swell took what remained up and over the rails. Dan clung to the rails and watched in horror as the debris disappeared into the blackness.

Dix ripped his jacket off his back and grabbed his mount's neck. He covered its head with the sodden fabric and kicked at the creature's legs until the animal went down into a kneeling position. Then Dix wrapped the sleeves under the horse's neck and tied a crude knot.

'Stay there, horse!' Dix shouted in a vain attempt to be heard above the eerie howling noise which surrounded the *Santa Catalina*.

The mount remained on its knees.

'What you doing there, Dixie?' Dan shouted above the sound of the paddle-blades as the entire wheel came out of the water and spun furiously in the air. A fraction of a second later the wheel came down hard into the hostile ocean. Chunks of wood flew like arrows as some of the wheel's blades shattered.

'Horses don't buck so much when they can't see, Dan,' Dix explained quickly into his pal's ear. 'Now

134

give me your coat. I'll try and do the same to your nag before the critter breaks its legs.'

Dan did not argue. He unbuttoned the water-laden coat and handed it to Dix.

Another wave hit them. This time it came from behind their shoulders. All three men were knocked down. They stayed flat on the deck until the water had gone back to the sea. Dix hauled himself and his two companions up.

Dix tried to rub the salt water off his face and screwed up his eyes until he could just about see. His eyes burned as if branding-irons had been poked into their sockets. He tried to fill his lungs with enough air to see him through his next task.

Then, like a puma, he threw himself at the horse. He hooked his right arm around the animal's neck and was lifted off his feet. The horse shook its head and neck. Dix was swung like a rag-doll but he hung on. His cowboy boots hit the deckhead above him before he and the horse fell heavily between the bull and his own mount. Somehow Dix's sheer stubbornness managed to subdue the winded animal.

The bedraggled man forced the wet sleeves through the leather bridle until the horse could no longer see. Dix gritted his teeth and used his entire weight to lengthen the sleeves until he could tie them together beneath the horse's chin.

'This is crazy, Dixie!' Dan shouted above the deafening sound. 'You'll get your brains kicked out by these critters! They're scared! Scared and dangerous!'

Dixie crawled across the deck through the water and dragged himself up beside the two soaked figures. Then the bruised and bleeding gunfighter turned until driving rain was on his back and his belly was against the rail. Dix looked out into the darkness and saw a huge wave rearing up like a defiant stallion.

'Give me ya jacket, Ramon!' he gasped. 'Only got Hickok's horse left to subdue!'

'*Sí, señor*!' Ramon nodded and obeyed.

Less than a second later another wave hit the boat. The sound of glass shattering along the starboard side of the vessel fought against the deafening noise of the angry sea. The *Santa Catalina* seemed to be pushed across the rolling waves. Then every timber in the vessel groaned as the front of the boat rose out of the sea like a rearing bronco.

All three men fell and slid along the deck through the water from one side of the boat to the other. Only the port railing prevented them from disappearing into a watery grave. Dix gathered up the slack in the rope which was tied around his waist and clawed himself back up on to his feet.

Dix inhaled deeply and charged at Hickok's tall

stallion. He tossed the wet jacket over its head and used the sleeves to tie a knot under the animal's head. He staggered to the port railings and stared out at the sea. The sound of thunder still resounded above the boat but the sea had suddenly calmed.

Dan and Ramon's fingers gripped around the metal bars until the paddle-steamer levelled out for the first time in nearly an hour. The few lanterns that still somehow remained alight continued to swing. Their flickering light illuminated the severe damage that the boat had suffered.

'Has it ended?' Ramon asked.

'Maybe. Maybe not,' Dix replied.

Ramon moved to the veteran gunfighter and looked at the man's face. Blood traced down through the weathered features.

'You are bleeding, Señor Dixie.'

Dix gave a muted laugh. He untied the rope round his waist and started to walk away from the aft end of the boat.

'Where you going, Dixie?' Dan called out.

Dix did not answer the question. He stopped in his tracks and stared to what lay ahead of the paddle-steamer. He was still glued to the spot when the sailor and Dan caught up with him.

'What's wrong, Dixie?' Dan asked. 'You look like you just seen a ghost.'

Tom Dix slowly raised his gloved right hand and

pointed at a wall of dense fog. The damaged *Santa Catalina* was heading straight into it.

'Look at it, Dan! It looks like it's alive!'

SIXTEEN

There was good reason for the mysterious wall of fog appearing to be alive to the three exhausted men at the bow of the paddle steamer. Suddenly the fastest twin-master in the Pacific Ocean cut its way through the fog like a branding-iron burning its way deep into the hide of a maverick.

The sleek *Black Serpent* sliced across the bow of the *Santa Catalina*. The pirates who hung on the rigging and manned the decks seemed to be equally stunned at the unexpected sight. The hunters had discovered their prey a long way from where they had thought it would be found.

Tom Dix gripped the arms of his two companions as the paddle-steamer turned hard to starboard.

'What the hell was that?' the stunned veteran gunfighter asked.

'Whatever it was, it had a big black flag hanging off its tail!' Dan gasped.

Dix led the men around the front of the boat to

where the twin-master had headed. The fog concealed all trace of the lethal vessel.

'A black flag?' Dix queried. 'What's that mean?'

'Pirates, Señor Dixie!' Ramon answered knowingly. 'Only pirates sail under the black flag!'

Dix and Dan looked at the small man.

'You gone loco, son?' Dix asked. 'Pirates? This is the nineteenth century! There ain't no pirates around nowadays!'

Suddenly, the *Black Serpent*'s oak bow sliced through the fog again. It sailed directly in front of the ailing boat. Dix, Dan and Ramon stared in stunned horror up at the line of cannon and the gruesome array of men which jeered at them. A fraction of a second later, the *Black Serpent* was gone again into the fog.

Even the first rays of the morning sun could not locate the lethal vessel's trail in the dense white clouds which hung over the sea.

'They're playing with us, boys!' Dan said. 'Why? What do they want?'

'The gold!' Wild Bill Hickok drawled as he walked out from the large dining-area. He rested his left hand on the rail and squinted hard into the fog. 'You boys forgot about the gold this boat's carrying?'

Dix rubbed the blood from his bruised features.

'Wild Bill's right!'

'But how could a bunch of pirates even know about it?' Dan asked.

Hickok turned. He drew one of his guns and pushed his friends out of the way. The huge boat had circled wide and was coming straight at them. The gunfighter pulled the hammer of his Colt back until it fully locked, then he raised it. He stood defiantly with his arm outstretched as the *Black Serpent* sped past their port side.

It was as if every pirate aboard the twin-master had fired at once. Deadly lead cut through the fog. The three men behind the broad-shouldered Wild Bill ducked. The heat of the bullets could be felt as Hickok repeatedly fired his pistol in reply.

At least three of the pirates fell from the gun deck into the sea as Hickok's brutal accuracy told.

'Good shooting, Bill!' Dan shouted.

Hickok holstered his gun and swiftly drew the other. The large sailing-boat disappeared once more into the sanctuary of the fog.

'You can join in any time you please, boys!' Wild Bill muttered. He turned and looked up at the metal stairwell which led to the deck above. 'I'm going topside!'

Dix drew one of his own Colts.

'You stay here, James Butler. Me and Dan'll go up and try and get us a better shot at them critters.'

Hickok's eyes narrowed.

'Kill the man on the wheel! This old boat ain't got a chance otherwise!'

The two ranchers nodded and ran up the metal steps. The sound of their spurred boots echoed over the gunfighter.

'What should I do, Señor Wild Bill?' the terrified Ramon asked.

'Get me a cigar and a bottle, son!' Hickok replied. 'Then hide!'

Bonanza Bob strolled out on to the deck with his guns in his hands. He eyed the tall Hickok silently.

'You better not turn them barrels in my direction, Bob!' Wild Bill warned. ' 'Coz if you do, you'll surely die!'

There was no emotion in the bloodied features of Bonanza Bob as he walked to the bow and turned his attention to the fog. He cocked both hammers and waited for the pirate boat to reappear.

'What in tarnation is going on here?' shouted one of the two soldiers as they came rushing towards the two well-dressed men with their rifles gripped firmly in their hands. 'What's all the shooting about?'

'We're under attack!' Hickok answered.

'Who from?' one of the troopers questioned.

Hickok raised his gun as he saw the black twin-master carve its way out of the fog again.

'From them!' Hickok said.

Like the wings of a flock of gigantic black vultures, the sails of the pirate ship flapped as its crew turned the long, heavily armed vessel toward its prey. The crew of the long vessel used their unmatched skills to keep the sails of the *Black Serpent* filled.

The well-armed Tall Red stood beside John Morgan as Curly Wilde swung the large wheel hard to port and steered the pirate vessel on a course which would bring it alongside the crippled paddle-boat.

No wildcat could have moved with more speed or agility. The *Black Serpent* was steered with unequalled mastery as the pirates in its rigging hauled the massive canvas up on the mainsail. Without the wind in its largest sail, the lethal twin master slowed down to half its original pace.

Both vessels were neck and neck.

Hickok fanned the hammer of his Colt and fired up at the *Black Serpent*. The pair of troopers and Bonanza Bob joined in.

Yet their bullets were no match for the thunderous cannons which exploded into action. The four men felt the paddle-steamer shudder as the hefty cannonballs tore the upper deck apart.

'Keep firing!' Wild Bill called out as he holstered his smoking gun.

The men obeyed.

Hickok raced up to the deck above. Wood smouldered where the deadly cannonballs had punched holes in the empty cabins. He tore the wreckage out of his path with his bare hands and clambered up to the highest point on the *Santa Catalina*.

Bullets shadowed his every step, yet he did not pause for even a moment. When he reached the wheel house he looked over the almost flat roof of the boat. The twin black stacks were still somehow intact and pumping dark grey smoke into the heavens.

'Dix! Dan!' Hickok called out.

The two ranchers staggered from the wheel-house to his side.

Their guns fired at the twin-master with every stride.

'They'll blow us apart, Bill!' Dan gasped as he knelt down to reload.

'No they won't!' Hickok vowed. He drew his Colt and aimed across the distance between them.

He fired.

The deadly shot caught the *Black Serpent*'s helmsman in the side of his head. Curly Wilde released his grip on the wheel and fell into a bloody heap.

The bigger vessel swayed violently.

Its wheel suddenly started to spin. The twin-master crashed up against the side of the smaller boat before it lurched and moved away.

Cannons blasted again.

The sea ahead of the paddle-boat punched white foam into the air as the cannonballs were sent drastically off course.

Pirates fell from the rigging and disappeared into the boat's wake.

'Good shooting, James Butler!' Dix said.

Without taking his eyes from the twin-masted boat, Hickok shook the spent shells from his bullet and reloaded.

'They'll be back as soon as they get someone else on that wheel!'

Dan breathed heavily. He watched as the *Black Serpent* came back under control and turned on an intercepting course.

'Here they come again!' He sighed.

Hickok looked at his two pals.

'Keep picking them off, boys. I got me an idea,' he said. He walked across the roof of the boat and descended the metal steps.

The sound of rifle fire filled both men's souls. Dix and Dan crouched down and watched as plumes of smoke came from the pirate ship. They could see the pirates firing at them. Then they heard the glass in the wheelhouse shatter.

The *Santa Catalina* seemed to stray hard to starboard.

'I bet the captain has been hit, Dixie!' Dan said.

'Go check, partner!' Dix said. He dragged back the hammers of his guns for the umpteenth time. He watched as Dan made it to the wheelhouse and entered before rising. He moved quickly across the roof of the boat and stopped behind one of the tall, black, smoke-stacks.

Bullets blasted all around him. Sparks ricocheted off the huge metal chimney. Dix inhaled hard and gripped his guns firmly. He knew that the twelve bullets in his guns were all that remained between himself and defeat.

There were no more bullets left on his gunbelt.

From now on, every shot had to count.

Hickok moved down to where he had left Bonanza Bob and the two army troopers. The gunfighter paused on the metal steps and stared at the two bodies beside Bonanza Bob Sherman. Their blue uniforms were bathed in blood. Blood that covered their backs.

Hickok dropped from the last step on to the deck. Bullets still tore into the boat from the pirates' guns as the twin-master closed the gap between them.

Instinctively Bonanza Bob turned with his smoking guns in his hands.

'Did you kill them soldier boys, Bob?' Hickok asked.

There was no reply. Only a smile which etched across the bruised face. His eyes told it all. He had killed the only two men between the box of gold coins and himself.

Hickok squared up to the man.

'I reckon this time we finish what we started, Bob.'

Sherman's eyes widened.

'There's enough for both of us, Bill,' Bonanza Bob said through broken teeth.

Hickok shook his head.

'No thanks. That gold got blood on it!'

Suddenly a hail of red-hot bullets rained down on them as the *Black Serpent* came within a few yards of the struggling paddle-steamer. The entire deck blasted into a million burning splinters. Then both vessels collided.

The impact knocked Hickok off his feet. He fell on to his back heavily and lay there for what felt like an eternity. Then he saw Bonanza Bob's chest explode as countless pirate bullets tore through him.

The man fell at his feet with a startled expression on his face. Wild Bill kicked the body away and scrambled up as even more shots tore up the deck. He moved into the large dining-area and met Ramon. The smaller man was standing with a cigar in one hand and a bottle of whiskey in the other. Hickok took the cigar and put it between his teeth.

'Where do you keep the oil for the lanterns, Ramon?' the tall gunfighter asked.

Ramon pointed to a door behind the long bar.

'In there, Señor Wild Bill! It is kept in there in barrels.'

Hickok picked a match from his vest pocket and ignited it with his thumbnail. He lit the cigar and puffed hard on it. Then he removed it from his mouth and blew the ash from its tip.

'Go get me a barrel of that oil, son.'

Ramon ran to the storeroom.

Then Hickok stared hard at the sight outside

the door opposite him. The side of *Black Serpent* was visible as both boats kept pace with one another through the deep waters. It seemed as if the two vessels were glued together. As Ramon returned with the small barrel of oil, Wild Bill pointed through the doorway at the boat.

'What's going on there?'

Ramon stared at it.

'They must have tied both boats together, I think.'

'Damn it all!' Hickok cursed as he turned with the barrel under his arm and the smoking cigar in his teeth. 'They'll swarm over us like ants if'n I don't do something fast!'

Ramon had been correct. The pirates had managed to sail so close that they were indeed tying the two boats together. Tall Red leapt across from the rigging and dropped down on the roof of the paddle-steamer. Within a heartbeat, a half-dozen more of the pirates had followed his lead.

Skin and Khan remained close to their captain as the others roamed across the top of their crippled prize.

Tom Dix had heard the thuds of the men's boots as they had dropped out of the rigging on long ropes. Without a second thought for his own safety, Dix rolled away from the tall black stack and started to fire.

Dix knew that he could not afford to waste even

one bullet and his deadly accuracy ensured that he hit what he aimed his matched Colts at.

One pirate after another was hit off the top of the *Santa Catalina*. Their lifeless bodies fell between the two vessels into the sea.

Khan fell on to his belly and lay there as his shipmates were knocked off their feet by the lethal .45s. He pulled his dagger from his belt and watched as Skin buckled beside him. The tattooed man rolled off the roof of the boat.

Tall Red ran to the cover of the other tall smokestack and cocked his Winchester. He then turned and started to fire. He pumped his rifle with unbelievable speed.

Dix was showered in hot sawdust.

He rolled backwards until his body was stopped by the six-inch-high brass safety rail. The rifle bullets trailed after him until the Winchester's magazine was empty.

Dix heard the sound of the rifle's hammer falling on the empty magazine. He raced for cover. He dropped down the stairwell and saw Hickok moving up with the barrel under his arm.

'What you doing, James Butler?' Dix asked as the gunfighter leaned beside him and peered over the top of the steps.

'How many are there left?' Hickok asked.

'A couple,' Dix replied. 'Maybe more.'

'We have to cut the ropes that them pirates have tied these two boats together with!' Wild Bill said as his gun grip broke a hole in the top of the barrel.

'What's in that barrel?' Dix asked.

Wild Bill used his long slender fingers to pull the bandanna from Dix's neck.

'Lantern oil,' he said through a cloud of cigar smoke.

Dix watched the gunfighter dip the bandanna into the barrel until it was soaked. He then pushed half the long cotton neck-scarf into the barrel and jammed it in the splintered edge of the hole.

'I get it.' Dix nodded.

Suddenly a volley of Winchester bullets blasted over their heads as Tall Red unleashed his rifle's venom once again.

Dan Shaw slowly opened the wheelhouse door a few inches and stared across at the twin smokestacks twenty feet away. He watched Tall Red blasting his rifle from the cover of the further stack. Dan cocked the hammer of his .45 and aimed at the pirate captain.

He squeezed its trigger.

The gun jolted as it fired.

Tall Red was knocked off his feet as the bullet caught him in his shoulder. He rolled over the flat roof of the boat as Dan fired twice more. One bullet hit the pirate in his side as the other flew over his head.

Tall Red was badly hurt. He dragged himself on to his feet, ran to the edge of the paddle-steamer and jumped. He landed in the rigging of the *Black Serpent* and screamed at his men.

'Lower the mainsail!'

Pirates released the mainsail as others cut the ropes which held the two vessels together.

Dan continued to shoot.

With renewed vigour, Hickok and Dix made their way on to the top of the *Santa Catalina* and moved cautiously to the smoke-stacks. Suddenly, as Wild Bill knelt with the barrel, he saw the massive Khan rise and charge at Dix.

'Look out, Dixie!' he yelled.

Dix turned on his heels just in time to see the pirate with his razor-sharp jewelled dagger in his huge right hand. He ducked as the deadly honed blade slashed at the air above him. Khan hit him and they both crashed on to the high roof.

'You kill many of my people, old man,' Khan growled. 'Too many me think.'

Dix rolled away from the gleaming blade but Khan kept on after him. He was fast for a big man.

Dix clambered to his feet. He ran a few yards and tried to aim one of his weapons. He stumbled.

Khan raced across the distance between them and lunged with the dagger in his hand. Dix fell on to his back and then slid until he went head over heels. He grabbed out blindly. His hands found the edge of the long brass rails that edged the roof.

Dix was hanging by his fingertips. His legs dangled in mid air and vainly searched for a foothold. Out of the corner of his eye he could see the huge sailing-boat moving away as wind filled its large mainsail.

'You die now!' Khan boomed.

Every sinew in Dix's body felt as if it were ripped from the bone as he pulled himself up until his head was above the wooden rails.

The sight of the huge pirate chilled him.

Suddenly two shots rang out.

A startled expression etched across the scarred face. Khan arched as bullets exploded from out of his chest. Tom Dix ducked as the huge pirate toppled off the top of the paddle-steamer and fell like a boulder into the sea below the dangling gunfighter.

Then a hand reached down to him. Dix accepted it and allowed Dan to haul him up to safety.

'You OK, Dixie?'

'You sure took your time, Dan!' Dix grumbled as he was dragged to safety.

Dan pointed to Hickok, who had used his cigar to light the oil-soaked bandanna hanging out of the barrel of lantern-oil.

'What's Bill doing, Dixie?'

'I ain't too sure,' Dix admitted.

Soon their question was answered. Hickok rose up with the barrel in his arms. He ran to the edge of the paddle-boat's rooftop and threw the barrel with all his might at the *Black Serpent*. The twin-master was still only ten feet away from the side of the paddle-steamer. As the barrel hit the mainsail, Hickok drew both his guns and fired.

His lethal accuracy blew the barrel apart. The flames of the burning bandanna engulfed the black canvas sail as the pirate boat veered away and into the dense wall of fog.

Wild Bill Hickok could see liquid fire as it dripped down on to the gun deck just before the pirate boat disappeared from sight. Even the fog could not hide the flames which had engulfed the *Black Serpent* as what remained of its crew vainly tried to fight the inferno.

As Dan and Dix reached the side of the exhausted Hickok they saw a half dozen huge dark shadows swim beneath the rippling waves after the blazing boat.

'Look! See them?' Dix said pointing down at the sea.

'Fish!' Hickok spat as he holstered his smoking guns.

'Fish?' Dix raised both eyebrows.

Hickok nodded.

'Big fish!'

A few moments later they heard the chilling sounds of strange creatures crying out in the heart of the fog. Then a massive explosion sent shock waves across the sea. The paddle-steamer rolled as the swell rippled across the surface of the ocean.

'What in tarnation blew up?' Dan gasped.

'Gunpowder, Dan!' said an unemotional Hickok. He turned and walked towards the metal steps. 'Them pirate boats carry a lot of the stuff to feed them big guns.'

Dix and Dan walked slowly after the tall gunfighter.

'What do you reckon them things were under the water, Dan?' Dix asked.

'Whales.'

Dix frowned.

'Not sea monsters?'

'Nope! Whales!' Dan insisted. 'Definitely whales, Dixie!'

Dix shook his head and frowned.

'You've got even less imagination than James Butler!'

FINALE

Kirby Jones was a big man both in sheer height and width. He had a smile that matched his nature. It too was big and honest. The man stood with a boot resting on the bottom rail of his largest Double B ranch corral as he divided his attention between the three mounted men before him and the prized white-faced pedigree bull he had just purchased.

'That bull will add new blood to my herd, Wild Bill,' Jones said. 'Reckon I'll be looking at a few hundred mighty fine calves come next spring.'

Hickok leaned on his silver saddle horn and nodded.

'Damn right, Kirby! That young bull's got vinegar, and no mistake.'

'Figure he'll have himself a better time here than he had on our old ranch, Mr Jones.' Dan Shaw smiled as he adjusted himself on his high Texan saddle.

'How many steers you got here on the Double B?' asked Tom Dix. His eyes darted around the

155

small portion of the cattle spread that they could actually see.

'Two thousand, Dixie.' Kirby Jones beamed proudly.

Dix rubbed his whiskers and grinned as he looked at the bull wandering around the corral.

'Two thousand? He'll definitely have himself a lotta fun here.'

Hickok glanced at his two mounted companions.

'Makes a man a tad envious, boys.'

'That bull will have to work darn hard to equal you, Wild Bill!' Jones winked.

'Yep! He sure will!' Hickok acknowledged. 'I sure hope he's up to the job!'

Kirby Jones stood away from the corral and raised his hand to the trio of riders. They each shook it vigorously in turn.

'I thank you boys for bringing this fine animal all the way here to San Remo,' the cattle rancher said. 'I'm grateful. I'm truly grateful.'

Dix patted his buttoned-down shirt-pocket where he had put the $800 in fresh bills.

'We thank you, *amigo*! Nice to do business with an honest man for once.'

'I second that!' Dan said pulling on his gloves.

'Ah, shucks!' Jones almost blushed.

'Don't get swell-headed, Kirby,' Hickok advised. His long fingers placed a thin cigar between his teeth.

'You boys riding into town to catch a boat back to civilization, Wild Bill?' Jones asked curiously.

Dix, Dan and Hickok all cleared their throats at the same time as they looked at one another and then back down at the hospitable rancher.

'What? Go back on another damn boat?' Dan shivered at the thought.

'Nope. We ain't ever doing that again, Kirby!' Hickok said firmly. 'There ain't nothing that could drag our sorry hides back on anything that floats!'

'How come?' Jones asked, squinting up at the riders.

'Boats ain't safe!' Dan nodded.

'They ain't?' The rancher shrugged. 'Then what do you intend doing?'

Dix stroked the neck of his mount.

'We're riding back to the heart of the West, Mr Jones!'

'All the way back!' Dan agreed.

Hickok struck a match and lit his cigar.

'Just think of all them towns between here and there, Kirby.' He sighed through a cloud of smoke. 'I'll bet that there's a saloon in every one of them. And girls prettier than any we ever set eyes upon. Yep, we're riding home.'

'See you, boys.' Kirby Jones lifted a hand in salute.

'*Adios*!' said Dix. He pulled his reins to his left, away from the corral.

'It's bin an honour!' Dan added.

Hickok touched the brim of his hat and turned his elegant stallion.

'Until we meet again, Kirby!' he called out over his shoulder.

The three horsemen aimed their mounts along the dusty trail away from the Double B ranch house and outbuildings. Hickok gripped his cigar firmly in his teeth and narrowed his hooded eyes.

'So you boys got a few bucks again,' Wild Bill said with the hint of a wry smile lightening his famous features.

'Thanks to you, old friend!' Dix agreed as he gripped his reins tightly.

'What you getting at, Bill?' Dan leaned forward and noticed the devilment in Hickok's expression. 'You're up to something, ain't you?'

'Oh, yeah!' the elegant gunfighter said aloud. 'I forgot to tell about something that happened back in town just after the *Santa Catalina* docked, boys.'

Dix and Dan looked at the smiling man who rode between them.

'What did you forget to tell us about, James Butler?'

'The reward money!' Hickok raised himself in his saddle and encouraged his stallion to gain pace as his companions tried to keep up with him.

'What reward money, Bill?' Dan called out as he drew level.

'The reward money the army gave us for saving their gold shipment, Daniel.' Hickok leaned over the neck of his galloping horse and taunted his pals. 'You boys were buying new trail gear when it happened!'

Dix spurred and caught up with the gunfighter.

'They gave us a reward?' he shouted.

'Yep!' Hickok used his reins to whip the shoulders of his stallion and then thundered ahead of his pals.

Furiously the two other riders spurred hard.

'How much money, Bill?'

'Yeah, how much reward money did they give us?'

'Catch me and I'll tell ya, boys!' Hickok spurred, looked over his shoulder and laughed. 'C'mon! What's wrong? You getting old?'

The three horses thundered away from the Double B cattle ranch with their masters standing tall in their saddles. They spurred on and on.

Wild Bill Hickok's laughter rang out over the sun-bleached range as he led his two friends into lands they did not know and back towards new adventures and a place known as the Wild West.

Home Library Service (For Staff Use Only)

1	2	3	4	5	6	7	8	9
		326A						

27094